Pauls

Pauls

stories
by Jess Taylor

BOOKTHUG
DEPARTMENT OF NARRATIVE STUDIES
TORONTO, 2015

FIRST EDITION

The production of this book was made possible through the generous
assistance of the Canada Council for the Arts and the Ontario Arts Council.
BookThug also acknowledges the support of the Government of Canada
through the Canada Book Fund and the Government of Ontario through
the Ontario Book Publishing Tax Credit and the Ontario Book Fund.

LIBRARY AND ARCHIVES CANADA CATALOGUING IN PUBLICATION

Taylor, Jess, 1989-, author
        Pauls / Jess Taylor. -- First edition.

Short stories.
Issued in print and electronic formats.
ISBN 978-1-77166-168-3 (paperback).--ISBN 978-1-77166-169-0
(html).--ISBN 978-1-77166-170-6 (pdf).--ISBN 978-1-77166-171-3
(mobi kindle)

        I. Title.

PS8639.A9516P38 2015   C813'.6   C2015-905695-0
                                           C2015-905696-9

PRINTED IN CANADA

Shelfie

A **bundled** eBook edition is available
with the purchase of this print book.

CLEARLY PRINT YOUR NAME ABOVE IN UPPER CASE

Instructions to claim your eBook edition:
1. Download the Shelfie app for Android or iOS
2. Write your name in **UPPER CASE** above
3. Use the Shelfie app to submit a photo
4. Download your eBook to any device

For Mom & Dad

Paul

ONE STREET OVER from Paul lives another Paul. They grew up together and are good friends. People sometimes describe them as inseparable, refer to them as "The Pauls," or just "Pauls" if they think they're clever. Paul who lives on Werther Street works at a paper mill, and Paul who lives on Spruce Trail Crescent became an academic.

When the two Pauls were ten, exchanging stories about bike rides and dirty jokes and secrets at the back of the playground, a third Paul was born to a family on the outskirts of town. Paul was a name that ran in his family – his father's middle name was Paul, and his grandfather's first name was Paul, and his great-grandfather's middle name was Paul, and his great-great grandfather's first name was Paul, and so on. A new Paul was born to the family, and the lights in the hospital hurt his eyes, and the air in the world hurt his lungs, and he wailed and wailed and that hurt his throat.

The two Pauls are twenty-five when this story takes place. One Paul has a stack of books in front of him, and the other Paul brushes fragments of wood from his clothes. New Paul is not so new anymore. He's fifteen. Paul goes to school, and he doesn't say much (perhaps part of him remembers how wailing hurt his throat). He comes home, and he goes outside, and he listens to the birds. And he walks into the forest, and he thinks about how every day is a new day, a good day, a strange day, and what a world it is that he lives in. He touches bark on trees. He touches the waxy surface of maple leaves and then touches elm leaves and tries to think about the difference. Sometimes he collects hickory nuts that have fallen onto the moss at the edge of the forest. He pretends to be a gatherer in a hunter/gatherer society, but he feels too old for such games sometimes. Those times he goes deeper into the forest where his cat emerges from bushes, and he follows her through the forest, mostly just to see where she'll go.

Paper-mill Paul has decided to get married. There's money in the bank, and there's a girl that loves him, and he's not sure what else to do since every day he drives to work and then he works and then he gets paid when two weeks go by and then he puts the money in the bank and takes the girl that loves him on dates and then he goes over to PhD Paul's house after he's drunk from dinner wine. And they stay up all night talking about the things they talk about and doing what they do. So Paul proposes and the girl that loves him accepts and starts picking out dresses. Paul sits in front of his computer reading literary theory, and he is alone, and his eyes hurt.

There's a girl in Paul's math class that has a crush on him, and she writes his name in the margins of her notebook, Paulpaulpaulpaul, and she tries really hard not to think about his last name. The way it would look after her first name. Besides, her older sister told her the other day on the phone from university that not all girls want to get married, and not all guys do either. Sometimes it's okay to not want those things and to be a Strong Independent Woman instead. And the girl thought that maybe that's how she should be. "But are we still able to love someone and be independent?"

"Of course. It's loving the right way. Still being your own person. That's what I have with Rebecca. Don't tell Mom."

So the girl writes Paul over and over and walks home behind him with wistful eyes. Paul never looks back. When the girl gets home from school, she writes different things about him, a boy named Paul. She remembers a Paul her mother once mentioned, one of her old friends; she remembers her sister once had a friend named Paul.

A Comprehensive List of Pauls

Paul - 15. Boy in my class. I like him. He sits across the classroom, and he's really good at math. The other day the English teacher called on him in class, and he didn't even hear him. He's always far away in his head. It's impossible for me to know where he goes.

Paul - 19. One of my sister's best friends in high school. They kissed once at the back of the soccer field, but then he moved away.

Paul - Deceased. Would be 50. Man my mother knew in university. He got very sick with ALS after he graduated. My mother gets really sad when she talks about it, and then she has too many glasses of wine and goes to bed early.

Paul - Fictional. 20. Main character in my favourite movie. The movie is beautiful - the colours all have a blue tint. It's about a young man, and he falls in love with a young girl even though he only ever sees glimpses of her (the side of her face, her hand brushing back her hair, her back walking in front of him) and follows her through the city, and eventually they meet on a bridge, and the sky is blue, the water is blue, the bridge is blue, even their skin looks blue. Blue, blue, blue. But then he walks away.

Paul - Fictional. 22. Character in a story I wrote. The story is too much like the movie. I don't want to talk about the story.

Paul - 35. First name of one of my teachers. My favourite teacher. I was in grade five, and he gave me my first adult book to read. *To Kill A Mockingbird*.

It didn't make much sense to me, but I liked the characters of Scout and Dill, and I liked the fact that he thought I was smart enough to read it, even though I probably wasn't.

After making this list, the girl isn't anywhere closer to understanding Paul, who he is, his motivations. The next day in class, she sends him a letter asking him to hang out after school. She chews on the end of her pen and watches as the boy next to Paul passes him the letter and points to her. She waves. Paul reads the note and searches out her eyes. His are a faded sort of blue (blue, blue, blue) that don't quite make contact with hers. He nods. She smiles, but he's already gone back to his work.

This time after school, she walks beside Paul instead of behind him. "I don't have very long," he says. "I have a lot to do tonight."

"Okay." With limited time to get to really know Paul, she starts asking him questions. "What's your favourite subject at school?"

"I don't have one really."

"Do you have any brothers and sisters?"

"No."

"I have an older sister. And my mom's going to have another baby soon. She says it's a girl, but Dad didn't want her to get it checked at the doctor. He wants it to be a surprise."

"Oh."

"Where do you go after school?"

"The forest. I like being alone."

"Okay. Well, do you want to grab ice cream or something?"

They are walking by the local ice cream parlour. Paul studies her again, looks her up and down, wonders what she wants. They order ice cream, and Paul pays for hers because his dad once told him to do things like that when you're out with a girl, especially in this town. It's the way things work. The girl almost doesn't want to eat her ice cream, studded with pecans and melting in the warm September sun, because it's special that Paul bought it for her. But she catches the drips with her lips, and suddenly has the feeling this might be the last time she ever eats ice cream in this uninhibited way. She imagines herself a year from now, six months from now, even a month from now, and that girl is different. She is nervous about getting dirty and dripping ice cream down her chin. She wants to be delicate and poised. The presence of the future girl makes the ice cream taste strange, and she licks it up. Paul crunches his ice cream cone sloppily with his teeth, and he tells her about a song he listened to the night before and how the guitars kind of sounded like light and there was a violin and it kind of whined like something sad in the background. He tells her because he wants her to listen to the song for some reason, but can't think of the song's name. "Anyway, I've got to go. It was cool hanging out."

"Yeah," she says, still thinking of the song that she'll never actually hear. And she knows that every time she hears a song with quiet guitars and violins that she'll think that maybe this was the song, and she'll think of the ice-cream, and being fifteen, and this moment with Paul. "Thanks for the ice cream."

And he waves at her and walks down the street, towards home. She thinks about going home herself, where her desk is waiting for her. Instead she waits for Paul to get far enough ahead, and then she follows him.

Paul rubs his eyes in front of his computer. He looks at his watch. It's only four in the afternoon, but he pours himself some whiskey. He's not sure he can handle reading any more words. Thinking about any more ideas. He has a feeling that his friend, who he will see soon enough, his friend who is also named Paul, has been hiding something. He drinks the whiskey and closes his eyes. He tries not to imagine finishing the PhD. He tries not to imagine teaching. Tries not to imagine fitting himself into academia, into finally settling down at a university far away from this little town that he keeps trying to leave and then coming back, broke and sad, to live in his parents' basement. Tries not to be jealous of his friend who is able to support his mother and pay the mortgage on the house one street over with the money he has made at the paper-mill. Tries not to think about the process paper goes through before it is made into the books that he studies and reads, and how many libraries and houses the books have passed through before this Paul, who is not even the one and only Paul, just another Paul, one more Paul, gets to read them. And he rubs his eyes again. And drinks more whiskey and listens to a song that he stumbled across on the internet with sad, quiet guitars and a violin that whines in the background.

Paul goes into the forest behind his house and licks ice-cream residue from his lips. Sun leaks through the roof created by the tree branches, and he calls his cat. "Cally! Cally!" His calico comes out of bushes with a meow. She waits for him to walk to her, and then she ducks under a low-lying branch. He follows her, grateful he's always been small for his age.

There's a place Paul likes to go when he's finished reading and working for the day, a special place deep in the middle of the forest on the edge of town. There's a clearing there. It's where he goes for a type of thought-clearing, a clearing for clearing. And after his thoughts are cleared, his friend comes to see him, and they talk about the paths their lives have taken, share their mutual pity. Paul is glad the clearing exists, hidden, in the middle of the forest, because sometimes Pauls need to find their own place to go and explore their connection, sometimes Pauls need to go somewhere that words and other people can't go. Some things are beyond words in a small conservative town. How much better it would be if Pauls were able to escape, make a new life. But Paper-mill Paul has to work, and PhD Paul will never leave really, never, not as long as Paul needs him.

She follows Paul, who follows his cat under brambles and vines crested with thorns that pull at her clothes and hair, but she needs to keep following, even as she skins her knees and elbows on the rough bark and branches.

The forest has hidden a system of tunnels that rabbits, cats, and small coyotes use to stay stealthy and secret. Paul feels contained, safe. They pass sumac trees, starting to blaze red with autumn. They creep under pine bows. Finally, Cally runs out of the network of branches and undergrowth into a clearing of tall grass. She runs across the clearing, along a path carved out by the hooves of herds of deer, but Paul stops. On the other side of the clearing, two men are standing underneath a grove of tall elms, and Paul thinks about the leaves on the trees. His cat runs to the men and, only for a second, glances back at where she's left Paul. Where he crouches, unsure, concealed by shrubbery.

The girl stops suddenly where she's been crawling along, and Paul can hear her and gestures for her to come sit beside him. She stays slightly behind him, and she listens to his breath and the way it catches, unsure, as if it's his first day breathing and it hurts his lungs and he's getting ready to wail, except he sits very still. His beautiful cat has disappeared into the other side of the forest. The girl sits cross-legged and watches the side of Paul's cheek. Where it moves as he breathes. Where his stubble is going to start coming in next year. She can see the day he is going to start considering himself a man, can see it in his cheek. She can see herself leaving the town, but she can't see what will become of Paul, it's a total blank, and Paul's faded blue eyes are steady, watching two men across the clearing.

One has his arm around the other one. The one being held removes his glasses and presses one hand to the bridge of his nose and the man with his arm around this man rubs his back gently. The man is saying something into the man's ear. Their cheeks are touching as one holds the other. Paul watches, and he imagines that the two men across the clearing, both their names are Paul, they've been named for the Pauls in their families that came before them, two more in two long strings of Pauls, and Paul is watching, the girl is watching Paul, as the two men embrace.

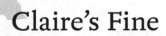

Claire's Fine

IN THE CARD SHOP, I was assigned Sympathy. "That's Claire's department," my boss said, and she put a hand on my shoulder like she was really giving me a lot of responsibility. I kept the cards in the section tidied, well-stocked, made sure orders were done, did revisions. Eventually my section expanded to include Get Well and Encouragement, and when a new line came out dealing specifically with Cancer Encouragement, my boss put her hand on me again and said, "In no time you'll be running this place."

One of the ladies who worked with me brought me a pastry for breakfast. "Are you all right?" she asked as I picked the chocolate off the croissant. "You've seemed down lately."

"Oh, yeah, I'm fine. I just haven't been sleeping too well."

"You aren't sick, are you?" my boss asked, wheeling her desk chair over to join in the conversation.

"I don't think so."

"Does your head hurt, sweetie?" my co-worker asked.

My boss put her hand on my forehead. "I don't know, you might feel a little hot. I can't have you working if you're sick. You'd better go home."

"I'm fine."

"Claire, believe me. I'm a mother. I can tell when someone's sick. Go home, get some rest. We'll handle your departments today. Call me so I know you are ready to come back tomorrow."

My co-worker wrapped the rest of the pastry in a paper towel and shoved it into my open backpack. Then she gave me a hug. "Feel better." I'd never had a boss be so unnecessarily nice before. Did I actually look sick? Maybe I was worn out, needed more sleep free of night terrors.

I wandered down the sidewalk, caked with snow. No one seemed to shovel or plough here, and nothing melted. One of the student newspapers was frozen in ice against the sidewalk. You could see charts and graphs depicting the number of assaults this school year. Sexual assaults. I didn't know why they couldn't say rape or what exactly it was that had been done. Everyone seemed scared to articulate it. Maybe it was for the best; once things are articulated, greeting cards are made. *Sorry to hear about your rape.*

When I finally got home, the fabric of my boots was soaked with slush, and my socks weren't only wet and freezing, they'd also picked up the dye from the insides of my boots so that my toes were stained burgundy. Nathan was at the library studying, and Paul was still asleep. The house was this still sort of quiet. I made tea, read a book, went back to bed after a while. It felt good to have no place to go, and to feel like, yes, yes, yes, you should be the one person who takes good care of you. You're all you need.

That night, the ice on the parking lot, it was almost like a skating rink, and I turned to Paul, and I asked him, "What're we doing at a strip mall on a night like this?" Snow falling from the sky.

"Eats!" he said, and then he used his boots to skid, flinging his arms out to steady himself. He grinned at me. "Close call!" He was always grinning at me. I was always telling him to knock it off. Nathan stood back and watched as Paul slid around. Then he winked at me, and, with a whoop, he ran after Paul, sliding and crashing into him. The boys fell over each other and laughed, Nathan pressing Paul's face against a patch of ice. I should've known they wouldn't act sane. "Claire," they shouted. "Come play with us, Claire!"

"I thought we were going to eat," I shouted back, but I was already sliding along the ice, hoping I wouldn't fall, or that if I did fall, one of the two of them would catch me.

We brought takeout to the house, flung containers on the table. North York was strange. I was used to the heart of the city, not the outskirts. I'd lived in the city for two years when I first moved out. I finished my last two years of school, renting a place on my own, and then I ran out of the money my Aunt Sofia had left me. I'd called Nathan, cried into the phone, "What am I going to do, Nate?"

"Get a house with me while I do my Master's!" So that's what I did. At first it was just the two of us in a little house in the student ghetto. Then Paul moved in, and the rent went down. I started working at the card and gift shop in Vaughan. I wasn't too sure what Paul did, but he was out at night a lot, and when I came home from work, he'd be up, drinking whiskey in the kitchen.

Noodles downtown are cheaper, less bland, and less greasy, but that night, it felt like the best food in the world. Nathan stretched out on the couch, put his feet on my lap. "Grab us some beers while you're up, Paul," he shouted and shovelled more noodles into his mouth. Paul was smoking by the open window, letting his noodles get cold.

"Oh, you guys," he said, but he was looking at me. I ignored him, my hand resting on Nathan's leg, and he eventually finished his cigarette, shoved the butt in a houseplant one of my girlfriends had brought me.

"Shut the window too, Paul. Claire's freezing."

Paul brought Nathan and me beer and drank whiskey straight from the bottle. "This is all we need, eh, guys. Just food, drinks, good friends." And he finally tore into the noodles.

One apartment that I had, back when I was in the city, had a rooftop patio, and Nathan and I used it to climb onto the roofs of stores beside my building, for no reason really, just to be on a roof. This was before either of us knew Paul, and Nathan didn't even go to parties like that

26

one where he met Paul, and it was always me and Nathan, me and Nathan, and that always made me feel good. The apartments were always after my aunt died - I can't really remember where I lived when she was alive except that it must have been in the house I lived in almost my whole life, with her, it must have been.

"You know," I told Nathan the first time we ever scrambled onto the roof, hoisting ourselves over the edge, "it's not like I think about the old house that much. But I just remembered that Sofia showed me the roof of the house. It was one of the first things she ever showed me."

"How old were you when you went to live there?" Nathan opened a beer that he'd brought up in his backpack and handed it to me. We clinked bottles.

"Oh, ten, I guess. The way out onto the roof, it was through my window. She said, 'I don't want you going out here alone, Claire, but I'm showing you the secret because I trust you.' And we walked out the window onto the sloped roof. We stayed out there looking at the stars. She wrapped me up in her coat when I got cold."

"She cared about you a lot. I can always tell, the way you talk about her."

"She was there for me when I needed her. I was hers."

"You were there too, Claire." Nathan meant the way I took care of her once she got sick. The time I took off school and work. But it wasn't enough.

"Yeah. I guess. Thanks, Nate." He could tell he'd upset me. I stopped talking and stopped drinking. And then we went inside. He curled on my floor in a comforter. I could hear the sound of his breathing as he slept. I stayed awake almost the whole night. We never talked about Aunt Sofia or that house again.

I didn't have to work the next day, and normally I would go and see Nathan where he worked at the library, but I didn't feel like seeing him. He was there every day, the one person I could rely on, and I kept thinking he wanted me to be this person I was before my aunt died, fun and excited, but every morning I found that I was someone different than I expected to be. So I stayed home, put some songs on, danced around the kitchen for a while. I wanted to make something really fancy for the boys, but all we had left was a little bit of margarine sticking to the sides of an old container, half a bag of perogies, and a bruised apple. So I boiled the perogies, then fried them in the margarine with pieces of apple. The smell woke Paul up. "What're you making, Claire?"

"Supper!"

"Smells good," he said. "What a good homemaker you are!"

I lightly punched him in the stomach, and he held it, moaning. "Misogyny is dead," I shouted. "Patronizing cannot exist without patriarchy!"

"Oh, it hurts! Why are you doing this to me, Claire?"

"Are you actually hurt?"

Paul stayed doubled over and nodded, and so I went to him and put my hand on his back. Then he turned his head towards me and grinned his stupid grin. "Just kidding." He slid his arm around me, even though he was still bent over, so low on my waist that it was almost around my butt.

"So how you been?"

"Fine." And his arm stayed around me. I tried to pull away. He held me tighter.

"No, I mean, how are you actually? You, me, Nathan, we hardly talk about anything."

"Sure we do."

"Sure. Okay."

"I mean, I'm fine. Why wouldn't I be okay?"

"I don't know. Sometimes you seem . . . What's it matter? Aren't you Nathan's girlfriend? It's up to him to check on you."

"I'm not."

"Aren't you?"

"No, not at all. I thought you knew that."

Then we heard the door open, and distracted, he relaxed his arm. I pulled away completely and went back to stirring my food. Paul straightened up like nothing had happened. Nathan came in, and he looked from me to Paul. I guess the two of us never really hung out without him there. "Hey guys." He gave me an especially steady look. "What are you cooking, Claire?"

"Use your eyes. She made us dinner."

"What's your problem lately?" Nathan asked him, and then he left the kitchen, slamming the door behind him.

"Well, that was uncomfortable," Paul said to the ceiling and then stabbed one of the perogies in the frying pan with a fork. "Guess somebody got his period."

"Are you guys fighting or something?"

"Who knows, Claire?"

This time, Nathan didn't come out to watch TV, and this time, the three of us didn't talk, and this time Paul didn't go out and I didn't go to sleep. Paul and I decided to stay up drinking together. I drank beer, he drank whiskey, and when we got really drunk, I started talking about my aunt.

"That's messed," Paul said. "I mean, that's so sad. I'd be sad all the time."

"Oh, I dunno," I said, but part of me wanted to say, I am sad all the time, even though it wasn't true.

We stayed up for a long time. Eventually I ran out of beers and started drinking whiskey and then I started leaning on Paul's shoulder, moaning, "I'm so tired, but I want to see the sunrise. Do you want to see the sunrise with me?"

"Of course I would want to see the sunrise with you, but I don't think you're going to make it, Claire."

"I'll make it. I know I can make it."

But I fell asleep on the couch.

Sometimes, as I lay awake in bed, I could hear the sound of porn coming from Nathan's room. Often it made me lonely and horny, but I just lay there, trying to block it out until I fell asleep. Other times the way the man yelled at the girl in the videos, the way he swore at her like she was dirt, made me think of all those girls in residence, the ones followed while walking alone. The newspaper girls. Girls passed out, drunk or drugged, statistics. How the ones murdered would never grow up to be in their sixties or seventies to live a slow, sad death. I never heard anything from Paul's room, on my other side, even when he was home.

I was on a streak of terrible dreams. Every night, I walked around at 5 a.m., hoping walking would jiggle all the bad thoughts out of my brain. Sometimes Paul was back by then, drinking whiskey from a mug in the kitchen, and he always watched as I paced, but he never said anything about it.

I called into work in the morning, once my alarm went off. "Hey, it's me. I'm still not feeling too well."

"Take all the time you need, Claire. You know how dead it is in January."

Nathan had slid a note under my door in the morning before he left, apologizing and asking if I wanted to come see him where he was working in the library. I thought about finding him and having a really chill day, just me and Nathan. But I ended up finishing a book while lying on the floor of the living room with a couch cushion underneath my head. Paul woke up kind of early and walked past me into the kitchen where he rummaged around, making coffee. He came out, holding a mug, and pressed his foot into my stomach as if he was an explorer and I was some rocky mountain he had just climbed and conquered. "Hey, Fruit Loops, want to watch the sunrise tonight?"

31

A lot of people die in the winter. So I knew that, the next day, I should be awake and alert for work. I should be ready to return to my duties, my various departments. Some die right before Christmas, but most die afterwards, right before spring comes. People slip on ice instead of using their boots as skates to glide across parking lots, and their feet skid out from under them and they end up hitting their heads. Then paramedics come and they are taken away, and then it turns out that they are hemorrhaging and go into the hospital and are in a coma and then their family friend goes into a card store and the friend gets a girl to help them find two cards. One is a nice Get Well card that the sick person will never be able to read because of the coma, so it will have to be more special for the family. And then the customer will need help picking out another card, one that is from the Encouragement section for the kids of the person in the hospital. Everyone knows that the person in the hospital isn't going to make it, so the card can't be too hopeful or say anything about a hard situation getting better. Instead it must focus on the inner strength of the kids and their ability to take these experiences as something that will make them stronger and more well-rounded people. And they are getting just the one card for the two kids (they aren't made of money) and the son doesn't like flowers or dogs, so it needs to have something else on the front. Maybe a cat. And then a week later, the customer is back, and they are now in Sympathy, and they want a Sorry for the Loss of Your Daughter Card for the parents and also a Sorry for the Loss of Your Mother for the kids, and during all of this chaos this week, the customer forgot to feed her son's hamster so she also needs a Sorry for the Loss of Your Pet, which is actually a good thing because it teaches him about life and death so that when his grandma goes, less explaining will need to be done. And then the customer will go to the cash and they have three cards so I'll offer them the Valentine's Day promo (the monkey swings its arms back and forth and says many charming phrases). My aunt died in February.

"Sure, Paul," I said. "We can watch the sunrise." I knew I wouldn't go to work tomorrow or the next day. I was never going back. Money meant nothing. Somehow I would afford to live. Nathan, at least, would take care of me. He always did. There was something strange going on right now that I was trying to work out, between him, me, and Paul. It seemed to all go back to where my room was in the house, the middle of the three, to how we spent time together, the three of us laughing and goofing around like three little boys instead of two grown men and a woman. Overnight Nathan had grown up and so had Paul, each trying to be more serious than the other, asking me questions, laying their hands on me, asking me, Are you okay? Because Nathan knew what time of year was coming up, and Paul wanted my full attention for some reason, the two of them pulling me from either side. Maybe they were still boys, maybe it was just tug-of-war and I was the rag stranded somewhere in between.

Nathan eventually got home, and I was in my room,

playing all my iTunes on shuffle. "Claire, can I talk to you?"

"I'm quitting my job."

"You what?"

Nathan stood in my doorway, and he watched me dance as my favourite song came on. "I'm quitting. I hate it."

"What about rent?"

"I have some money saved. Don't just stand there. Dance with me!" He came into my room and kinda bobbed his head at me and danced in a very contained manner, hardly moving his feet. "You needed to talk to me?"

"Oh, never mind, it's not important." He smiled at me and looked into my eyes as we swayed side by side.

I wanted to tell him, I don't understand you and neither does Paul, but I didn't. We kept dancing until we got hungry, and then we all chipped in for pizza. Paul stayed home all night again.

He brought out some weed and rolled a joint, and we all opened the window and took turns breathing smoke out into the thirty below night and took bites of pizza when it wasn't our turn to inhale. "I'm going to take a power nap," I said.

"What about the sunrise?" Paul had the joint sticking out of his mouth and was sitting on the kitchen counter.

"Don't worry. I'll set my alarm for two hours from now," I said. "And we'll resume this party."

"What sunrise?" Nathan said, and he looked from Paul

to me. "Paul, get off the counter. I don't want your ass where I cut vegetables."

"Like you even eat vegetables."

They convinced me to hang out a little and watch TV before I finally went to lie in my bed. I could still hear the voices of the boys, and the sound was a gentle hand that rubbed my back until I fell into a sleep free from nightmares.

When I woke up, the house seemed darker than before I'd gone to sleep, even though we had already turned off most of the lights in the house. I dressed and started to walk back out to the kitchen. I guess I've always had quiet footsteps. My aunt used to say that I terrified her almost every second with my creeping around. Even if I tried to stomp, it never made much noise. And then she would just laugh and hug me, even though a second before she had shouted, "Claire! One of these days you're going to kill me!"

The boys were still talking, it sounded like it was just about some party Paul and Nate were going to that I hadn't known about. But then I heard Nathan say to Paul, "I want to talk to you about something."

"Shoot."

"I want to know what's going on between you and Claire."

"Nothing."

"Oh yeah?"

"Well, nothing so far."

"Look, I just really want you to know, be careful,

okay? I know the way you are, and she's going through a really hard time."

And Paul said, "You think I don't know that? You think I walk around the house with my eyes closed? You aren't the only one that knows her." I heard Nathan put his beer bottle down on the counter.

I walked into the kitchen, and they stopped talking. Nathan hugged me. "Hey, Claire, you made it," he said.

"Yeah, see, Paul? No sunrise yet!"

"You're right, you made it." And Paul laughed and exchanged a look with Nathan. I was their little secret, and all those things they said about me.

Fine is a funny word. The weather can be fine. There can be fine stitching on clothes. Fine can mean small, contained, delicate. Fine can mean okay, all right. Comme ci, comme ça. When someone asks, How are you? You can say, Fine, and mean the opposite, or you can mean, I am like a careful line of stitching, how are you? You can mean, I am delicate. Be careful that I don't get snagged and unravel.

We drank and drank. Nate's never been able to drink much without it making him tired, but he was trying to fight going to bed. He leaned his head against the kitchen cabinets, while I rambled on about the three of us moving to Europe. "Seriously, guys, I'm so done with North America, it's dead here. You know what we should all be? Jazz musicians! Nate, quit school, and Paul stop doing whatever you do, and I'm already quitting my job, and we'll all just become these really hip jazz musicians, except sometimes we'll do a weird fusion style and then we can be known for innovative improvisation."

"Claire," Nathan said, his eyes still closed. "None of us can play instruments."

"So? So?"

Once Nathan fell asleep, slumped on the counter, Paul and I lifted him together and walked him to his room, Paul taking most of his weight. Paul stumbled back out to the kitchen to fill his glass with more whiskey. I pulled off Nate's shoes and jeans and pulled the blankets over him. "Thanks, Claire." I lay down beside him, over top of the sheets.

"No problem, Nate."

"How are you?" he mumbled through the sleep that was starting to catch up with him. His eyelashes were so long and dark, they brushed the edge of his cheek.

"I'm kinda drunk."

"Me too."

He wrapped his arm around me, and I lay on his chest for a bit until he fell asleep. I lifted his arm off and set it beside him. "Night, Nate," I whispered.

"Ni," he said.

"You took awhile," Paul said when I returned to the kitchen. "What took so long? You give him a goodnight blow job?"

"Why do you have to be so gross?"

"It's part of my appeal."

37

"What appeal?"

"Oh, leave me alone," Paul said.

"I'm not doing anything."

"You're right. You're not. You know what I think about you, Claire? Part of me thinks you are one of those people who is constantly having a breakdown, constantly moping around with that little frown on your face, but it's so long and drawn out that hardly anyone notices. You just really want someone to notice."

"What does the other part of you think?"

"The other part thinks whatever you want me to think."

I should've been annoyed with Paul, all this time I should've been annoyed with Paul, Paul who always had money and weed and alcohol, Paul who was usually never home late at night when he told me and Nate he was working but never told us where. I should've been annoyed, but mostly I was relieved. Like finally, I could just stop. I could stop pretending.

Once I saw her in a dream, about a year after she died. She put her hand on my shoulder and told me not to cry, that everything in life would eventually be okay and that this was just the way things were and it would all be fine in the end. I never told anyone about that. Not even Nathan. I wanted to tell Paul then, but the way he was smoking that cigarette and staring out into the sunrise - finally the sunrise! - his eyes were so far away, who knew what he was thinking about, or if he'd even have heard me.

Earlier that night, after the pizza and the weed and before drinking in the kitchen, the three of us had sat in the living room watching TV and the news came on and we were all too lazy to change the channel. Nathan had his eyes closed on the couch beside me. Paul sat in the chair, watching me, as the announcer reported that another girl had been sexually assaulted on the university campus. I don't know why it affected me so much, if it was the approaching month or the drugs or what, but there had already been so many this year, and each one seemed worse, more terrifying than the one before, and I walked past newspaper boxes back when I had a job to go to, and they were always right there on the front page, and then they'd been in that school paper, frozen in ice, assaults in charts and graphs and numbers, and Paul watched me sob into my cupped hands.

"Maybe you're right," I said.

"Maybe. What are you going to do now that you're done your job?"

"I don't know. Maybe just read. I wish I knew how to do something. I want people to think I have a bleeding soul, that I offer some sort of unique vision. I want people to see what I see, and I want them to go, Wow, wow."

Paul passed me his cigarette. "I've always thought that. Since I first met you, Claire," he said, and I didn't believe him. I couldn't. He emptied the whiskey bottle into our glasses and shot his back. He leaned on the counter, staring out the window. The whole kitchen filled with orange light. "Now, that's a sunrise."

We Want Impossible Things

We Went Impossible Things

I HAD A HARD TIME falling asleep because I knew I couldn't possibly be pregnant with his baby. And yet I was four days late, according to the app on my phone, and there was a gnawing in my stomach, like she already had a mouth.

Everything gets caught up with everything else. This fall was an echo of every fall that came before, and this him, the one that might have gotten me pregnant, was more or less an echo of the first him. And the first him was more or less an echo of certain men in my family. People for whom when I was obedient, I was the world, but the rest of the time, most of time . . . well.

I didn't want to take a test. I had taken tests before and they never really told you anything. Besides, it was just four days. Four days was a blip, it was nothing, but when I fell asleep behind my eyes I could see us becoming a new family.

In the morning, I lay on my bed and tried to forget my past or to remember it as something true, reremember it as honourable suffering. I imagined everything I'd ever done had been leading up to this moment. My bad decisions were not bad decisions; they were something fated and filled with the tenderness that I contained. What was happening with this baby inside me, it meant something. She was important. She would be everything I couldn't, everyone would love her, she would change the world and fix all of the things that were wrong with everyone. I would no longer rage out or get into a dark place. She was meant to happen.

The reason why I wasn't on the pill had to do with the first him. Being on the pill made my breasts grow, and my stomach. Also I just wasn't seventeen anymore. Also I was filled with a strange flatness of thought that made me need too much food and sleep for twelve-hour intervals. I used to be smart, but then I couldn't speak, at least not without complaining. When we stopped having sex, his dick a floppy nothing in my hand, I'd cried. "Is it because I got bigger? Is it because I gained weight?"

He thought for a second. "You know, maybe. That probably does have something to do with it." So I quit the pill. But then when I stopped it, I looked at him and he was still him, so I quit him too. I moved to the city, where everything glows, and I lost weight, but not the upset. That's what twisted and grew.

Sometimes I dreamt of people rubbing off my skin with sand. They said my name as they did it, the way the new him did during sex. "Paulie, Paulie, Paulina." I still hadn't had the heart to tell him everyone just called me

Paul, although he should have realized with all the mutual friends we had. For some reason, I thought he'd get weirded out. He once ranted about names that were ambiguous, not hinting towards a gender. He hated Taylor and Aidan and even Lesley. He liked to call me Paulina because it meant I could have a baby and that every time we had sex it was a risk. Especially since like most men I've met since leaving the first him, he hated the tight, latex second-skin of condoms.

We had a pack of the same friends, and after a while I started noticing him, or he noticed me. Everyone else was in couples anyway, and it seemed the most natural thing for him to walk me home as everyone was hopping into cabs and then sleeping together. And then I didn't hear from him until the next time everyone got together for drinks. But it's not like it mattered. I was well versed in the one-night stand, and at least this wasn't a one-night stand. Or maybe it was just a series of one-night stands. We couldn't get along, which was a problem, and we were getting to the age where people didn't just want sex, they also wanted to find the perfect companion. It wasn't enough to find the person *interesting*. They also had to be funny, and kind. They had to not make you angry and not get too angry with you. Especially when all the couples were composed of best friends, people with similar interests and perspectives on life. And several times when I started talking, he'd just walk away and be by himself at the bar.

I don't want you to think life was empty. I valued those friendships. There was a spark of something I'd been missing before. I taught children art in an after-school program. About colour and expression and shape. They showed promise, a peculiar way of looking at the world. It gave me hope for them, the way they'd grow, even if I didn't have much hope for anything else. During the summer, I grew a garden in a plot of land at the back of my shared house. I read all day sometimes, when I wasn't working. Things that had happened to me before moving to the city had left me raw. And reading, just like when I was a child, along with my friendships, seemed to be the way to fix it. I was learning. I could feel myself growing every day into a woman. And it was maybe not an easy thing. But it was a special thing.

We were hanging out with my friends, and I kept ordering soda water, saying I had program prep to do that night after I got home. Everyone always commented when anyone didn't drink, as if they were playing it safe or were a borderline alcoholic, or hated all of their friends.

I was a good friend. It was the only thing I really knew how to do. It was why I was good at the after-school program, the same skills. It wasn't very hard. When they wanted to hang out, I was available. When they had secrets, I was there to listen. When they needed help, I was there to lend a hand. I offered them surprisingly little of my personal life - none of what had happened with the first him, what my scars were from, the problem with

The Cousin. People only saw my smile and the wild golden hair he liked to gather in his hands and lift from my neck. I wasn't quiet - the opposite. But I had rules about what was okay to talk about.

It was the end of the night, the moon was shining its pretty face on down at me, and we were alone on the back patio. Our friends were all inside buying drinks, he wanted to smoke, and I wrapped my coat around my body making a little bundle of self. He wasn't talking to me, even though we were alone, and finally I said, "You know, you're the one who's always stressing me out!"

And he didn't say anything because he didn't want to get in another fight, but I felt his baby knee me from the inside.

"Look at that moon," I finally said, and I was sick of doing all the talking even though that was the way it always was and what he said was one of the biggest problems with me. Along with my lack of honesty. Along with how loud I was. Along with my pushy nature. Along with my moodiness. But he was moody too, just maybe in a different way. I was able to laugh in the middle of anger. He was able to be angry in the middle of laughter. Was there a way for me to keep the switch flipped on? Stuck on love? It never quite got there - flicked from hate to strong like then back to hate. I wanted him to put those big hands on my stomach and then on my face. But we all want impossible things.

"It shouldn't be this hard," he said, and that wasn't like him at all, caught up in the quiet defeatism of the world.

And of course, that made me snappy. "How else would you figure it all out?" Part of me said, *You're making a bad decision again. You're provoking him.* But my scalp was on fire and more than anything I felt I deserved to be alone.

Our friends came back outside to the patio, but the bar owner flicked off the outdoor lights to let us know it was last call. All I could see was his ember in the dark, glowing as he smoked. And the moon. My friend sat beside me, and she started crying quietly. I just held her hand because I knew her mom had died, and my mom was alive and my friend was drunk and who cared that this baby was growing in me - his baby - belonging to him who didn't give a fuck.

I never was the kind of girl to be direct. I was too shy about my own feelings, although I was so full of feelings, and sometimes they all spilled out of my mouth. I knew girls who would blow up the phones of their boyfriends or girlfriends with texts, girls who would follow their infatuation around, girls who would drop by his or her work, girls who screamed outside of their houses. I never did those things. I respected boundaries. And my intensity already branded me a crazy girl, so I had to keep my distance. But I thought, *If this is a baby, if she's really alive, then I should be able to go to his house.* I ate four slices of leftover pizza so I wouldn't have to eat in front of him, and I walked from my neighbourhood to his in the early afternoon, the leaves coming down and getting stuck in my hair. *How romantic*, I thought, and then I had the intention of telling him. That it was now a week late, and we were going to have a kid because I wasn't so sure about an abortion. Also this would mean that we'd have to figure things out.

He answered the door. "Oh. Why are you here?" He was wearing sweats and had obviously been working on writing. He smelt like coffee and pulled me into a hug.

"I have the day off. I wanted to see if you wanted to come for a walk."

"You know you can call me ahead of time, right?"

"I was in the area."

Calling him made me scared. Sometimes I texted and he didn't answer, so I didn't text much. I expected him to shut the door and say, *I've got work to do. Don't bother me at home.* But instead he said, "Were you, now?" and picked me up and carried me over to his futon where he pulled off my clothes and pulled me on top of him, and once again I didn't ask about protection. Afterwards, he dressed quickly and walked on over to his fridge, pulled out a beer. I trailed behind him, buttoning my shirt, my favourite one, with rows and rows of stars.

Beside his sink were several half-drunk glasses of milk. "My roommate," he said. "Sorry." I opened the cupboard looking for a glass for water, but there were none. "Don't you want a beer or something?"

"It's early," I said.

"Well, wash a glass then." I dumped glass after glass of milk down the sink. The yellow-white clumps hugged the holes in the drain before getting rinsed down. I washed all the glasses, as a present. I tried not to think too hard about the milk. "Did you actually want to go for a walk? Or did you get what you came for?"

I filled a glass with water and drank it, then filled it again. "Well, with all this free water, your house seems the ideal place to be. But I thought a walk would be nice."

"I *offered* you a drink. I have more than water."

"I'm joking." I walked over to his bookshelf and examined his books, Hemingway lined up beside Hemingway. "Hills Like White Elephants."

"What about it?"

I shrugged. He kept looking at me and sipped his drink. I chugged another whole glass of water.

I stopped looking at his books eventually, and we spent time walking around his neighbourhood, admiring the old trees, and I wanted to just bawl and kick at him and run down the street without ever looking back. I knew he'd think that made me childish, but what else was I supposed to do? Everything was so easy and perfect between us this day, but the next day he'd hate me again, and all I'd be able to think about for a week would be his baby and his hands. I grabbed one of them, and he pulled it away. "Come on, we're *outside*," he said.

"Hills Like White Elephants," I said.

And a change came over his face. "Why don't you just go home?"

"What." I knew he knew.

"Go home and get out of my life. You're constantly pushing. Showing up at my house, playing your games.

Stop whatever you're doing."

"But." And I started to gag, it was rising up in me, the baby and the pizza and the glasses of water. I thought about milk, the disgustingness of milk.

"Are you really going to throw up right now?"

"No." I took a deep breath, the way my therapist suggested to do when my scalp started to tingle, so I wouldn't start yelling or punching things; my knuckles already had too many scars. But he never gave me time to calm down. He was already walking away, he wasn't looking back. My hand was still warm from where it'd tried to hold his, but soon, walking home with the skin bare, it burned with cold.

Something was wet between my legs. I climbed the steps to my apartment, and I hated him. And autumn. God, the stupid mouldy leaves. The hallway inside my house was dark. I imagined an ember floating in front of me, lighting the way. My love's cigarette. It was the first time I'd ever thought of him as that - my love. But he didn't love me - who could? - not even full of his DNA.

My apartment was too cold. The radiators hadn't been turned on. I went to the bathroom, pulled down my pants, my underwear. Oh, red. Moist and red. I leaned my head against the tiled wall, my hand tearing toilet paper into strips. They littered the floor. I listened to the drips.

Breakfast Curry

I WAS ALWAYS EATING breakfast curry back then. Waiting for a world that wasn't this world and also for my wound to heal. It was my platelets. It had nothing to do with the breakfast curry, although I can see how you might make that connection. The details of breakfast curry and the wound being so close in proximity.

I call it breakfast curry not because it's actually a special curry made for breakfast. It's a dinner or lunch curry heated up in the morning. Or eaten cold right out of takeout containers. My mom had gone veggie, and she'd suggested I go veggie too, and I always listened to my mom. Sometimes I still try to listen to her, even now. I was living above a dry cleaners in the north end of the city, and there was a curry place next door. They had a ton of veg options, and the owner told me stories about immigrating to Canada and marrying his wife. I told him about my accident, about needing to leave work. He accepted my ten-dollar bill and handed me the change. He told me that his son hadn't got into any universities in Ontario, but got into one in British Columbia and was moving to a whole new part of the country. At first, he'd thought it was a failure, but now he felt a fresh sense of independence. "See?" he told me as he bagged a free veggie samosa. "Beautiful things are unexpected."

I texted my old girlfriend. Just to touch base. It didn't matter that we'd slept together and had one drunken conversation where I suggested getting married, right around the time we broke up. I mean, I think it didn't matter. **What's up?** she wrote back. **Wanna Skype later?**

Skype usually meant sexy Skype, but I didn't really feel like it. **No. I want to talk.**

Oh. Okay.

I'm sick, I told her.

Okay.

I've got a chronic illness. I flexed my hands. They used to always be covered with oil, sore from a day of work, but now I hardly did anything at all.

What is it?

It's in my blood.

That can happen?

My body won't heal.

Can I come over?

My joints hurt, I typed. **Sometimes I bruise. There's a wound on my leg. I haven't been going to work.**

Can I come over?

I stood in front of the mirror in the bathroom. The cell was hot in my hand. I waited a few minutes. I knew she'd be staring at the screen. **If I get cut, you know,** I smiled at myself. I rubbed my stubble. **the bleeding might not stop.**

I started to dream about being cruel to people, twisting their arms, spitting on them. And infinite girls, pushing and squeezing and bending girls every angle they could possibly go, all while pressing myself into them as they resisted. I was a nice enough guy in real life, but I started to wonder. Maybe I was bad, you know, in my core, something a little off that made my immune system spoil. I knew I was thinking about my body all wrong, or at least my buddies thought I was thinking about my body all wrong, like it was connected to the soul, whatever that was.

I was 25 when it happened. I'd just got my first job as a junior machinist, and Jeremy, Will, and I would get drunk every day after leaving the shop. We were in some bar parking lot, and Jeremy and I were goofing around, wrestling right up against cars - he was this big bear, and I was this scrappy little thing. And then I fell. Or he knocked me down. A broken beer bottle punctured my leg. We pulled it right out, and I didn't even yell, but then it started gushing and gushing. "That's gonna scar up badasss!" Jeremy said.

"Paul, man," Will said, "we gotta get you to the hospital."

The doctor sewed up the gap in my leg, and said I should come back in a week or so to check on the healing progress. Well, there was no healing progress. The thing was so sore, I had to take time off work and started popping T3s. "I'm disappointed in your progress," the doctor said when I went back, like it was my fault or something, like I'd been slacking on the job. He sent me to get bloodwork done, as if I needed more things stuck in me, and that's when we found out about my platelets.

I didn't even know there was a glue in your blood, that shit that made scabs and helped you heal. Mine were low, low enough to warrant being monitored, but not so low they wanted to shoot me with steroids. "We might need to," the doctor said, "if that wound on your leg doesn't heal."

My mom started Googling ITP, the thing that means your platelets are always going to be that way. "Stop drinking," she told me over the phone. "Vegetables should be good for it. Start exercising."

"Mom, how can I exercise with a gash in my leg?"

"Go for walks. Rest. Stress can be a factor. Do you feel fatigued?"

I took more time from work and walked around the neighbourhood in the morning and taught myself how to cook beets. I stopped drinking.

"What's drinking got to do with your damn leg?" Jeremy asked.

"When you coming back to work?" Will added.

They couldn't understand, and I wanted to do a shot just to shut Jeremy up, but I also wanted to be someone with principles and liked the idea of not dying too young.

I liked the idea of avoiding whatever had helped stop my dad's heart. I tried to put it into words they'd get. "Guys, I've gone for four blood tests now. That gluestuff is low every time. You know what my mom says that could mean? That I'm chronically ill. CHRONICALLY ILL."

"Like cancer?" Will asked.

"Your mom doesn't know anything," Jeremy said, and I wished my leg would just heal so I could beat him down to the ground.

I started thinking that maybe my skin wasn't the only thing torn up. Everything started to look a little different. My mom came over, and we ate beets together, and she told me about my brothers, how they were doing with their wives, their jobs.

Even though I was 25 and I was chronically ill and there was a part of me that wouldn't close, these things brought on such a sweetness in my mouth. Like cold curry in the morning or the purple stain on my fingers from peeling beets. Fall trees and then snow and then new leaves. Cold food takes on a different taste, the tomatoes sweeter, the paneer saltier.

"There's a wax," my doctor told me. Four months in, no work. "I still don't want to give you the steroids. They'd be hard on you." He explained that the wax would go in the wound, and then my body would absorb it like stitches. The hope being that it would help me heal from the inside-out.

Will and I stopped hanging out with Jeremy so much; he was dating a new girl, and whenever we saw them together, she'd have a cut or bruise near her eye or a puffy lip. We never said anything, we just stopped calling Jeremy. Will and I still got together, and I told him about my mom, how she wanted me to see a healer.

"A healer? Really?"

"Why not? Nothing else helps. There's no real cure."

Will smiled, but didn't say anything and ordered another beer. I was still off booze. I took him home in a cab, sloppy and drunk, heat coming off his breath that fogged up the chilled cab windows.

The healer I went to was this shiatsu guy. He said he'd ask me all sorts of questions and if anything felt too close that I could just block him out by saying, "No," either out loud or in my thoughts. He went through my organs, one at a time, by feeling the air around me. He stopped every so often when something stuck out to him, when he felt a blockage, pain, or something that just wasn't right.

Sometimes to fix ITP, they remove your spleen. I didn't quite understand it, but my doctor told me sometimes the spleen gobbles the platelets up or hangs onto them, keeping them from going where they need to go. I'd gone in for an ultrasound. They squeezed gel on my stomach in a dark room. The woman didn't look at me - she looked at the monitor and rolled a plastic thing over my abdomen, and it didn't hurt, but it was very hard and very cold. I tried to see the monitor, but she didn't angle it in my direction. One day, I thought I'd be in the ultrasound room with a wife, looking for a baby's nose, listening for a little heart beating. But immune diseases were genetic. Maybe I wouldn't even have kids.

"Kidneys, gallbladder," the healer said. Sometimes he breathed in deeply, like what he was finding was viscous and hemorrhaging, but then he moved to another organ. The ultrasound woman had felt for my spleen, my stomach, every internal part of me.

"It's your emotions," he said. "In Eastern medicine, spirit and body come together. Your emotions are putting a strain on your immune system."

"Oh." I didn't know what all to say. I'm not an overly emotional guy. I've never really been in love, I don't think, at least not that kind of crazy love people talk about. The only reason I was even there was to respect what my mom thought was a good idea, putting all my faith and trust in her, nothing else.

This strange tinkling music was playing, a whispering soundtrack. "When you were young, did something happen to you?"

I said I didn't know. And I didn't. It could have been any one of six hundred things. My dad. How my older brothers locked me in rooms and closets. When my oldest brother's first girlfriend decided to teach me how to stroke a girl. It could have been all those things, or none of them.

"Your relationship with your father?"

"Distant."

"And your mother? You care a lot."

"She raised me and my brothers almost singlehandedly. She's wonderful. So brave. So smart."

"Something happened to her. You were fifteen. It made you more attached."

"She fell. Down stairs."

Dad had pushed her. I knew he did. Bruises blooming all over us in secret. Her head smashed against the tile floor, blood spreading toward the bottom step. I put my hand to her face, her open mouth, and my hand came back wet.

"That was positive for you."

I learned I could take care of the family, of her. I helped make dinner, did laundry, rolled together pairs of socks for her, my dad, my brothers. It taught me I could be responsible. My older brothers didn't care the same way.

The shiatsu guy told me I had to let go of something that was holding me back.

He said, "I'm going to work on balancing your immune system today. I'm going to put balls of silver and gold all over you, on your pressure points, and it'll balance you. Right now, your immune system is out of balance, like a tire deflated on a bicycle. We need to pump air in one tire and let air out of the other tire."

I had no idea what he was talking about. He left the room, and I undressed. For the first time since I was a teenager, I really examined my body as I stood there, waiting for the healer. The wound still there in my leg. I had some bruises on my knees from ages ago. I could feel my ribs on my torso. I wanted to be healthy.

The healer reentered. "I wanted to show you my wound," I said. I lifted my leg for him to see, propping my foot on the chair. It had a sheen of pus on it, yellow bruising all around. I quickly wrapped the bandage back around it, so it wouldn't make both of us nauseous.

"That looks painful," he said. "Thank you for showing me. I'll avoid it."

The healer pressed the gold and silver dots into my pressure points and then leaned on my body with all his weight. When I was little, my parents used to hug, and sometimes, I'd get in between, hugged from both sides. But that's what it felt like, having the healer's body on top of mine, pushing his elbow into my kinks.

After the massage, he asked me, "I picked up something about your father. Where is he?"

"Dead."

"Do you want me to try to communicate with him?"

I hadn't signed up for something magic. I hadn't been looking for an answer like that, or expected this man to go digging around in the emotional junkyard that was my family. "Whatever."

The healer closed his eyes. One hand cut into the air. He started laughing and looking like he was talking to someone in the room, moving his mouth without making any sound. I sucked at my lip, waiting. He opened his eyes.

"So?"

"I reached him."

"What did he say?"

"He made some jokes."

"Did he . . ."

"He didn't have a message to send you."

"Figures."

I paid the healer seventy-five dollars and left. Silver and gold balls were stuck to my body with adhesive. I picked each one off as soon as I got home, tossing gold and silver balls all over my apartment floor.

Eventually I let my ex come over. After we had sex, she lay on my chest in a new way - she used to roll over and face the wall, fall asleep as soon as possible. She held my arm, she kissed my neck. "Do you ever think about it? About, you know, after?"

She once told me all serious relationships start with three Very Serious Talks: 1) Past relationships; 2) Alcohol and drug use; and 3) Religion and worldview. We never talked about any of those things, so I'd assumed we'd never gotten serious, despite the way I sometimes held her face while we kissed. And I'd never really talked about that stuff with anyone, except maybe my mom right after my dad died.

"Nah," I said.

"I'm sorry you're sick," she said. "I wish you weren't. I think about you all the time."

"Let's go to sleep."

And she was quiet, but stayed lying on my chest. I knew I'd never be able to call her again. I expected to have a vision then, or a life-changing dream. I expected to feel something different, but instead I knew I had to get her out of there as soon as possible in the morning.

Between the restaurant and my apartment door, I saw it. My wound hurt in a different way, as if it'd changed to green, even though the spreading bruise was still a dark yellow-grey. The edges of my vision vibrated and broke into fractals of colour. The sky was so blue for November. Spots of red burst into the sky, a spinning dome of white. And then empty sky, cutting blue.

While I was eating, I really thought about it and it made sense that perhaps I'd been overly hungry, or it was a side effect of my illness or the pain. I'd never believed in UFOs or spirits or even a god. But some mornings, I did feel the clench inside me, the hope that if I was running toward an early death, something would be waiting for me.

That night, Will and I walked along the lake, and I thought about the white floating dome and the lights and the healer and my ex and my mom and even beets and curry, but I couldn't begin to tell him about it. The lake looked like a dark pool of ink, or maybe even blood, nothing reflecting on the still water.

The sky filled with a tremor and a burst of light crackled through. Red and white, there a second and then gone. Just light, unexplained, crackling, and true. "Did you see that?" My hand grabbed Will's arm. "Man, did you see?"

"Looked like lightning," Will said, shrugging me off.

"But doesn't lightning go down? Shouldn't it have hit the lake?"

A rumble and crack sounded throughout the sky, and this time a white shock touched the lake, and the light spread across the surface of the water over to us. Part of me expected the electricity to jump onto the shore and shoot into our bodies, to cure me of ITP and fix whatever Will hated most about himself. It fizzled out, the lake hissing with steam.

"Was that normal?"

Will didn't say anything, stayed with his eyes on the sky, waiting for more light. The light never came, and we walked back up to his apartment building. I lay on the couch in his bachelor, and he read me the Wikipedia article on ball lightning. As he tried to explain what we'd seen, his room tilted in my head and I had to shut my eyes. I listened to his voice describing electricity and knew I'd never have another friend who would stand by me and watch as liquid became gas inside of a static minute.

I went in for surgery. They injected me with steroids to get my platelets high enough to go through with it and put me under. They cut away the dead skin, they shot my wound full of wax, I woke with the gap in me filled, but I still felt that breakfast curry sweetness. My mom was there beside my bed, and she smiled at me as I came to. It healed, but my levels stayed low, but not too low, and then soon I was back in the hospital, but instead of in the bed, I was beside the bed. Sometimes I climbed in and tried to hold her fragile body to me. I wanted her to know I loved her. I was grateful, and her skin was thin, the sky cutting, the hospital clean.

I haven't grown old yet, and there's always the possibility I might not make it. The world could split open, the sun could go out. You should hear the way Will talks now since his first wife died, like we're all teetering on the brink of disaster.

Jeremy was right though. It did scar up badass. I go for walks along the lake, close to where I now live, watching for light, and wonder if any glass stayed in me, if the curry place is still in business, what colour my bruises will be tomorrow.

Multicoloured Lights

PAUL COULD STILL SEE the lights from the club reflected in her bathroom mirror. She turned on the faucet and ran her hands under the water, feeling her skin contract with the cold. She put her fingertips to her forehead, attempting to ease her headache. It was nothing she hadn't experienced. As far as anyone could see, she was safe. She was in her own bathroom, protected. She caught her eyes in the mirror and tried to focus on them, and then it came back to her in flickering snippets, something she wanted to tear out of her head like an annoying roll of unravelling film, plastic negatives slicing into the edges of her skin as she pulled. She climbed into the empty bathtub and held her knees. Stef would be there soon.

Stef stood behind Paul, set her hands on her shoulders and squeezed them, not knowing it was the wrong thing to do. Paulina tried to catch her mirrored eyes again. "I always knew something like this would happen to me." Stef had found Paulina crouching in the bathtub, her hands pressed against her face, but nothing wet coming out. Poor, poor girl. Poor, careless girl.

"Paul, it's not like it was meant to happen. He's just some sadistic asshole."

This was definitely the wrong thing to say. Paulina pulled away from her friend's hands, where they still strained to comfort. She pulled her hair away from her face and tucked it over one shoulder. "It doesn't matter. It's stupid. I didn't even get assaulted. Not really." But Paul knew, from her dreams, from the way things always went, an assault would eventually come.

They first met when Paulina moved to Toronto. Stef had brought her daughter, Wynn, to a Mommy & Me art class. Most Mommy & Me art classes at the facility were geared towards infants drooling over their paint-covered hands. This one was specifically for ages five to seven, a bonding experience for mother and child. Wynn liked to paint and draw, but she was silent the entire lesson. Stef had her at twenty and was constantly trying to prove she could have a good job and have a good relationship with the man she lived with, and was A Good Person. Paulina came around, assisting the children and parents on their projects. She introduced herself as Paulina, but said everyone called her Paul. She seemed like the good person Stef wanted to be, the way she helped the kids cut out shapes and gave each student, parent too, her full attention. At the end of the lesson, as Wynn continued to spread glitter-glue over-top her picture, Stef ended up confiding in Paul about her silent child, asking about ways they could bond through art even if Wynn was withdrawn. Paul had told her that she was new to Toronto, and Stef said, "Well, now we're friends!" And she meant it. Real friends.

Stef brought Paul into her friend group, and Paul started spending time with the people she met there, even when Stef couldn't get a sitter. But Stef did have a sitter the night that it happened, and friends do not let bad things happen to friends.

Stef could still remember the way her mouth had tasted the morning after losing Paul. The soft mildew texture of her tongue. The alcohol smell. She'd rolled over and hovered her fingertips across her boyfriend's naked skin. He didn't wake, even with her non-touch sliding over his back. She'd come in at 3 a.m., had texted Paul that she hoped she'd made it home from the club safe. But Paul hadn't made it home safe. Stef had gone over as soon as she'd heard, right away, leaving Derek to watch Wynn, had let herself in with the key Paulina had given her, and found her in the tub, as if it was the only place she'd ever belonged, a water spirit without water. And she couldn't say the right things, she couldn't believe she had lost her the night before.

Stef's boyfriend was watching soccer when she returned. "All okay?" he said without looking up.

Stef wanted to tell him about what had happened, but how can you explain that? *Last night at the club, Paulina went missing and it turns out something bad happened to her and I can't believe we lost track of each other and I should have*

73

called the police instead of coming home and why do things like this happen can you tell me why men do things like that or not even men just people in general do you know how to make it stop you were here with Wynn and didn't even hear me when I got home how powerless are we is there a way we can make sure this never happens to Wynn what are my responsibilities in this why can't you do something don't you know I count on you?

And Stef was dedicated to getting along with the man she lived with, and this was sure to start a fight. "Yeah, all's okay. Paul's just a little upset."

"How come?"

"Who knows? You know how Paul is." Paulina never talked about herself. Not her feelings. As much as Stef had wanted to take Paul in her arms, she couldn't understand what she was thinking.

Wynn was playing with plastic dinosaurs Paul had given her by the television set. Stef got down on her hands and knees in front of her daughter. "Hi."

"Hi."

"What you playing?"

"Attack."

"Listen."

"Yeah?"

"I want you to always tell me if something is wrong."

"'Kay."

Someone scored a goal, and Stef's boyfriend hollered from the couch. Stef moved to make sure she was out of the way of the television screen.

"Like even if you just feel wrong, and like you have no one to talk to."

"'Kay."

"You have me to talk to. Always. Tell me. If you think something bad will happen. Or if something bad has already happened. I'm not going to be mad, I promise. Even if you think it's something wrong. You can tell me."

"Mom, a pterodactyl is biting your ankle."

She hugged her daughter and held her the way she'd wanted to with Paulina. "Always, always feel like you can talk to me." A commercial came on, Derek's attention turned to Stef and Wynn, and the three of them decided it was best to go out to dinner that night.

Perhaps he'd taken pictures of "her perfect body," as men liked to call it as they slapped, and slapped. Maybe the cause of her nightmares was that she didn't know what had happened. She had found a man at the club to kiss and dance with, the music creating a beat behind their gyrations and sweat-covered bodies that she could mistake as the start of love. She had lost sight of him later in the night, and Stef had come dancing beside her. "Do you really like that guy?"

"Sure," Paulina said, but she knew it was the music she liked and the dancing and the lights, the way they shone patches of colour across the floor and sometimes across her skin. But she did like him. She did.

The thing was, she was unharmed. And this was almost more confusing than if she had been cut up into pieces and left all over Toronto.

It all got mixed up in her head as she read a psychology article about BDSM and how being submissive was a choice and being dominated was okay if that was your preference. But how to know if submissive truly was your preference if it was just always what you were expected to be and, in your sex dreams, you were neither, just a coming, fleshy blob, not man or woman, just energy that fractured into multicoloured lights, like the ones in the club. Maybe the best way to have sex was just to be drugged to sleep, while someone watched you, mesmerized by your stillness.

It's time to go, she told herself, and took transit to the hospital where she explained what had happened, the drink she drank and not knowing who she was when she regained consciousness, the experience of loss, how she had been found and was lucid within minutes, still missing her clothes. The sexual assault worker asked her, "And you're sure there wasn't an assault?"

"I don't know what happened."

She took her from a waiting room with couches and chairs, made to feel safe. In another room, she was handed pills, just in case she had contracted chlamydia or gonorrhea from him. She swallowed them and tried not to throw up. She peed in a plastic sample jar, but the sexual assault worker told her it would probably come back negative. "The drugs leave your system so quickly. Even if you went right after it happened, it probably would still not show up. You black out for about 3 to 5 hours and it's already gone by the time you're conscious. I'm sorry."

"You don't need to apologize," Paul said and handed her the jar.

She spent her days with the doors locked. The curtains drawn. Fascinated by his obsession, she Googled the name of a cousin who had claimed to love her, wanted to marry her, touched her, had sex with her, tried to kill her, tried to kill himself, and caused her first pregnancy scare all before she was fifteen. He'd moved to Vancouver years ago - the restraining order her parents had placed made sure they didn't contact each other, but she tried to find him sometimes, through the safe distance of the internet.

Except it was impossible to be safe, people were everywhere, all over the streets. Paulina couldn't help smiling at them all as she watched them glaring into the screens of their smartphones or pacing quickly towards a job they hated. Someone should smile at them, but there was something about this open way that her friends chastised. "You're asking for trouble, Paul." But Paul wasn't naive; she knew people are always pressing, they are always everywhere, there's always something they want.

Stef went to meet Paulina the day after the day after at a café near to Stef's. "I went to the police station," Paul said. "I feel kind of stupid talking about it. How's Wynn? How are you?"

"What happened at the police station?"

"The usual things," Paul said and sipped her Americano. Stef had never been to the police, not even after the things that had happened with Wynn's dad. He'd just disappeared, and she'd started teaching college, proud of herself for being able to support Wynn on her own. And then she'd met Derek and learned to count on someone again. She had wondered for a brief moment if she should call the police after Wynn's dad had left. If she should steal Wynn away in the middle of the night to protect them. "Nothing will happen. There's not enough proof. The officer told me, 'As far as we know you guys could have both just gotten retarded-drunk.'"

"Are they allowed to say retarded?"

"Well, she did."

"Maybe you should complain?"

"It doesn't matter." The café suddenly felt too small. She didn't want to cry in public, not when Paul should be the one crying. "I'm just trying to figure out how to go to work tomorrow."

"Maybe it will make you feel better? To see the kids?"

"I'm teaching Daddy & Me. How stupid is that? Parents that want to get their kids into art lessons before their motor skills are developed. I'm just sick of it."

Stef had remembered the way Paul used to describe her work at the art centre, her private art lessons. She had told her there was something about the kids that gave her hope. "Are you feeling really bad today? Are you okay?"

"I'm just sick of working all day with kids whose parents want them to be special. They expect them to be artistic geniuses. And it's not because they want their kid to be an artist. That's the last thing they want. But they want their kid to show that they are the best parents, magical almost with their ability to give their child the money and guidance and private lessons they need to develop their gifts and become a special kind of well-rounded." Paul paused and downed the rest of her coffee. She remembered being five and being held by the first person who claimed to really love her. Eight years old and her cousin. "But none of those children will ever be special, or an artistic genius, or anything. Or maybe they all will be geniuses, I don't know. Another genius, a product of money and private education. Another unique child exactly the same. The real special kids are the damaged ones. The ones that won't speak to you because what's in their head is already beyond their comprehension. Because they've seen things or had things done to them or done things that have messed them up. But they don't get paid attention to, maybe because they are too poor, or because people don't realize that when bad things happen, that makes you special too, and not even in a bad way. Just in a different way."

Stef thought about Wynn and her games, how quiet she could be staring out the window. She thought about Wynn seeing Stef get shoved against the wall before her father walked out for good. Did she absorb it? Was it in her too? Had Stef let Wynn down, just like she let Paulina down, and none of the worrying, the pacing in front of her door at night, would ever undo the moment Stef had chased Wynn's father into the street, where he flagged a cab and called her a crazy bitch and then got into the cab and was never heard of again? She'd smacked her hand against the roof of the cab as he drove away. Fractured her hand in two places.

"I'm sorry," Paul said. "It's just been a hard couple of days. Of course I'm still going to work. I love it."

Stef now couldn't properly hold back the tears and so she said she needed to get home to Wynn and marking. The two women hugged as they parted.

Wynn was entranced by something out the window. Stef cut up celery sticks in the kitchen, watching. The way Wynn moved her head when she caught sight of a bird, a yearning cat in a little girl's body. "What's wrong with you?" Stef thought. Had she watched birds in the same way? Had she been quiet the way Wynn was, disappearing for hours in a closet or under a bed, or even on the living room chair, not even reading, "Just thinking, Mom."

She brought the snack into the living room. "How much blood is in a person?" Wynn asked. The dinosaurs were still tossed by the television, but Stef was too tired to get her to pick them up.

"I don't know, Wynnita. A lot." Stef went to her bedroom, lay down, and let the tears come.

"Hey, what's the matter?" Derek asked.

"Nothing, nothing, nothing," she said.

"I have to go to softball. Did I do something?"

"No, it's not you. It's just the world."

"How can you be sad about the whole world?"

"I just am."

"The world's too big to be sad about." He kissed her at her hairline. "I'll be back in a few hours. Call me if you need me home . . . I'll skip the drinks."

"It's fine, just go."

She could hear Wynn rummaging around in the living room. After two hours, she put out dinner and then went back to bed. She let sleep ease the tension from her eyes, neck, calm the ache that was developing in her chest. She thought about her mother and wished she were there. She could use a cool hand pressed to her forehead on a night like this.

His name had been ordinary, yet Paulina, of course, remembered at the police station. Another Paul. They'd joked about it, Paul and Paulina, what a couple. But that was before he took her home, and then a gap, and then Paulina not remembering she was Paulina, in a hallway, naked.

Her nightmares were slow and long. She wasn't able to move, pinned to her bed or maybe her limbs were incapable. She had read about sleep paralysis, but this wasn't that - where you woke but couldn't get up - this was paralysis within sleep. Men stood around her bed and took out bags of sand. They passed the bag around slowly, while Paulina tried to get her mouth to work, begging them to stop. Each man took a limb of hers in their hands and pulled it to the side, straightened it to its full length. They put her fingertips and her toes in their mouths and sucked, then they bit. They gnawed away her skin until blood ran along the bed and onto the floor. Then they used the sand. They ground it into her fresh wounds and along her skin until it was raw and peeling.

In the morning, she texted Stef: What a night, and now, off to work!

Stef texted back, How are you?

Paulina typed, I'm not sleeping right, and erased it. She wrote, Fine, and erased it. She wrote, Stef, can you sleep here tonihgt and something about the spelling mistake made her start to choke on tears, or no, it was her cousin's hands around her neck when she was twelve years old; it was the men in the nightmares, hands covered in sand; it was the fact she couldn't move and she knew he was watching her, but didn't know what he wanted, and Paul clicked send.

Stef texted, Of course. Do you need me now?

Paul wrote, I have to go to work. How can I look at the kids?

Stef said, Cancel your class. It's not worth it.

I finish at five. Come then?

You got it.

Paul left the house, and the eyes of the people on the street followed her. She got on the streetcar and flashed her metropass and she was still being choked by those hands. She felt her lip to check it wasn't fat. She'd forgotten to brush her teeth. Somehow she'd packed her art supplies for the class, but when. The streetcar slid to a stop at the subway and everyone crowded for the doors. The person who sat beside Paul pushed past her. Paul couldn't tell if it was a man or woman. She didn't even look. She remembered how to use her legs and she was back in the hallway moving like a mind outside a body, drifting. *I need to escape.* The doors at the bottom of the stairs provided a way out, but Paul looked down and realized she had a body and it was naked. *If I am naked, I am more likely to be attacked. I can't escape that way.* She went up instead to the top of the staircase and pounded on doors. It was six in the morning. And a woman spoke to her through the door and Paul couldn't make words properly, and finally the woman took a chance and let her in and gave her clothes, and then Paulina went home and thought about it. Put together the pieces. The club. The man named Paul. His apartment. Kissing. Drinking the drink. The hallway. Nakedness. The doors. The woman. But why? Why, when they were already kissing? Already in his apartment? The gaps made more gaps and then more gaps. She imagined him sitting by her naked body, just watching. Spending the whole night watching.

She walked down the steps to the subway and walked back up them. She walked back down the steps to the subway and tugged at her hair. She thought about buying a coffee. She forgot if she had her metropass. She thought about all the dads and their children and how they were waiting for her, to watch her and follow along and paint. To stare and copy her every movement. So many men trying to be like Paulina.

She got back on the streetcar. She texted Stef, **Screw Daddy & Me. Come now.**

83

Stef called her sitter. "I'm sorry it's such short notice, but Derek doesn't get home for another two hours." She packed an overnight bag, texted Derek the details of what happened, finally. She would be there for Paul and make everything better. It would be as if it all never even happened. Their friendship was so strong.

As she headed through the living room, she tripped over something. A dinosaur tail smeared with red goo. Wynn was on the carpet with a bottle of ketchup. Some dinosaurs had been chewed through with scissors, their halves and dismembered limbs scattered across the floor. Others had their mouths clamped around the stomachs, legs, or tails of their dinosaur friends. Some stood mouth to mouth. To Stef they appeared to be kissing, like the massacre was actually some sadistic dinosaur orgy. Wynn squirted ketchup over everywhere they had bitten. Scales sticky, scarlet red. "Wynn!" Wynn stopped squirting the ketchup bottle. "What's wrong with you? What are you doing?"

"I'm playing attack."

Stef ran to the sink and grabbed a roll of paper towels, wet a bunch, and threw them overtop the decapitated dinosaurs. She came back in the room and grabbed the ketchup bottle from Wynn and threw it into the kitchen sink with a bang. Wynn winced at the sound and curled into a ball on the floor. Back in the living room, Stef took a garbage bag and stuffed the dinosaur parts into the bag. Wynn started rocking on the carpet. "What is wrong with you? Wynn, don't you know things like this actually happen? People get attacked. It's not something to joke about. It's not funny, Wynn. Now you have no dinosaurs left."

Wynn wailed, the sound muffled by the carpet. Through her howls, Stef thought she could make out Wynn's saying, "I'm bad." *No, you're not. I am.* Stef put down the paper towels and cradled her hunched body. She held her until her tears stopped and then held her still when the babysitter came in and said, "What happened here?"

Stef said, "The world." And the three of them cleaned up together, and then Stef went off to be a good friend to Paul.

The thing about friends is that even those you've known since childhood will still be a mystery. You can hear their words, you can hold their hands, remember the details of their past, believe what they are telling you. But you'll never know all of it. What else is chattering away in their brains. What they are hiding from you.

At Paul's house, Stef and Paul didn't talk about it. They locked the door once Stef got in, and Stef made tea. They watched movies and read each other their horoscopes and talked about Wynn and talked about the future and talked about outer-space and talked about a rare bug that had been found in the Amazon rainforest and talked about life with Derek and talked about teaching and talked about how much they missed clear nights away from the city (so many stars) and talked about how Paul once tried to learn how to smoke and failed and talked about their parents and talked about art and talked about books they had read and talked about this lecture Stef had seen on the internet, and then they went to bed where they lay head to toe.

Stef lay awake and wondered about her life. How she was twenty-five with a five-year-old daughter she didn't understand and was a college instructor and was probably doing everything right, but was so scared of doing something wrong. Or of all the wrong things in general. A murmur rose through the dark. "I am a full human. I am a full human. I am a full human. I am a full human." Stef reached out for Paul, but couldn't find her hand.

Wishweeds

THERE'S A TYPE of weed that grows here - I think it's pretty common - they grow tall, a leafless stalk, and at the top there's these yellow flowers that look like splayed-out suns, the sun a little kid might draw. We used to look for them at the edge of the forest behind my house. They go to seed like dandelions, but the seeds are huge, their white-grey parachutes almost as big as the palm of my hand. If you blow away all the seeds from a dandelion, you get a wish, just one, but with these weeds, each seed is a wish. Stace called them wishweeds. She was always better at finding them.

Stace used to decapitate Barbies when we were eight. I'd walk on down the street to her house all on my own. My parents thought, in this town, the empty roads meant you'd always be safe, especially if you were in grade three and had a vocabulary like I did. Besides, my baby brother had just been born and was constantly giving my parents a talking to. She kept an empty popcorn tin, the type her family got for Christmas, three feet tall, filled with Barbie arms. Their heads and bodies went straight in the trash. Stace didn't need them. We'd go out onto her front lawn, the manicured green so different from the wild ground-cover that composed ours up to the woods. Stace would run all over the lawn, shoving the bases of the arms into the earth as I picked flowers and stacked them into a pile and then crushed their blooms with my fingertips, pollen staining my nails. The little plastic hands protruded upwards. Wrists bent at pageant-delicate angles. As if they were dead bodies reawakened in the earth, or cheerleaders trying to high-five the sky.

"What the hell happened to your shoes?" Stace and I are sitting on top of the washing machine. Concrete peaks through the chewed up linoleum floor, and I'm scrubbing my pink high-tops with a toothbrush. The pink is stained with mud. We bought those shoes in the mall together – the first time my parents trusted us alone in the city. They cost sixty bucks, and they made my feet feel like I could go anywhere, I had my own colour and style, I could escape anything. And of course, first week wearing them, they are ruined.

"Do you think bleach will get it out?"

"Not if you still want them to be pink."

"I ruined them with Brad." We climb off the machine and throw the shoes in, hoping the wash cycle will make a difference.

"What? How?"

"We made out, okay? In a swamp."

"Well, that was dumb." Stace kicks at the washer. "That's so typical Brad." Like she knows Brad because he kissed her behind the portable when we were all eleven. Truth or dare.

"I don't even know," I say, and it's getting hard to speak. The washer rocks, creaking the ugly linoleum. I kick at it like Stace. The pain in my foot works.

We don't really talk about much, sitting on the laundry room floor. She doesn't drill me on the make-out session. I think her parents might be splitting up, and I wonder about the arms she pushed into the earth, if one was ever forgotten and then pulverized by a lawnmower. Instead of talking, we play the story game. We each write two lines and then cover the first. The next person has to continue the story without knowing all that's been written. The story gets grosser and grosser, more about sex and cum and cocks. Things I know Stace has never seen. She used to grab wishweeds and say, "I wish for . . . a man." And then she'd wink at me like she knew what that meant and instead of giving me a wish, she'd keep them all for herself and blow the seeds into the air. I think part of her thought they'd all morph into men in the air, perfect hair and plastic bodies, life-sized Cool Shaving Ken dolls, ready to rescue us and take us away from this town. But I always knew better. That wasn't what wishes were for. We switch my shoes into the dryer. They are still stained. I can hear the rubber soles thump thump thump, as if the shoes are alive, begging to be set free.

Of course they shrink. The fabric. Stace goes home and I shove them to the back of my closet where my mom won't see them, and then I cry. Once I get started, it's like I can't stop, and I hate Stace and I hate my shoes and I hate the mall and I hate that there are wetlands in the middle of the forest. Even lying down pisses me off, so I finally grab a book in an attempt to distract myself, but my thoughts are static.

"Jill, can you go outside with Paul? He doesn't want to play alone." My mom ducks her head into my room, and I straighten up.

"I used to play alone all the time. I'm busy." She made my bed this morning with the bedspread I've had since I was Paul's age - crescent moons, bites of moon-cheese missing, eaten by a cosmic mouse that lives somewhere not on the comforter.

"You don't look busy to me." I go outside, after throwing my book against the wall, so Mom knows how annoyed I am. "Hey! That's not like you," she says, and I want to growl, but I just make sure the screen door bangs back into place as I go out.

Paul ducks through the wire fence that separates our land from conservation, and then he's off into the field. I hang back, press into a grove of sumac trees that borders the fence. I lean against one of the spindly trees - Stace and I used to spend hours sitting and talking in them - but it cracks with my weight. Paul runs back, braces a foot against a crook of branches and reaches to grab ahold of one above him. In a moment, he is up where the blazing red leaves are and swings from one tree's branches to another's. "I'm a spider monkey!" he shouts. "Jill, be a leopard that wants to eat me!"

"I can't today."

"Please! You did it last week, it was so fun. Chase me!"

"No, Paul, I'm not a leopard today." I shake the tree that he is in, and he screams with fear and delight.

"Oh, you're a monster today!"

I keep shaking the tree and shaking it. I can't even see. Paul screams and laughs louder and louder, and then he lets himself drop from the tree and bolts out into the field, shouting, "Look out! Monster! Monster!"

I pick up a stick, hard and stubby, I'm barely able to get my hand around it, it's so thick, and I chuck it after him. The snap of my arm stings. My whole body. The thump sounds like a sneaker in a dryer, and he falls to the ground. All I can see is the field's long grass.

"Paul!" I run to him. He sits up and starts wailing. I gather him into my arms, my little baby brother. Alone in a nest built of long sweet grass. "I'm so sorry, I'm so sorry. Are you okay?" He clings to me, even though I was the one that did it.

"Yeah, but it hurts." He touches the back of his head.

"Please don't tell," I say as I smooth his hair. These words aren't mine. Too automatic. I kiss his forehead, right at the part of his hair. "Please, please." And Paul presses further into my shoulder. "Please, Paul, I love you. Don't tell on me. I was just being the monster."

Brad took me into the forest. He held my hand. He's tall, and his hair is dark, and out of all the girls he chose me, even though Stace had liked him since we were eleven. I thought that meant I was worth something. We started to kiss against a tree. His back pressed bark, and he pulled me into him, pushed his crotch into mine. His dick hard as it jabbed my hip. He gave a little moan, and I wondered how that could possibly feel good – I was sure I'd get a bruise. He pushed into me harder, so I gave a little moan too. Still kissing me, still with his arms around me, he started to back me into the clearing. "It's muddy." I had to pull my mouth away from his. He covered it right back up with his mouth, and then he wrapped one of his legs around my leg, so that I had to let myself down to the ground. He pulled at my pants, and there was mud in my hair and on my cheek. "Stop," I started to say, but then I remembered that Brad's my boyfriend. He pulled off my pants, there was mud everywhere, I moved my head to the side and looked into the long grass. It stung. My whole body. Two of us hidden in a nest built of long sweet grass. And I saw them – in a cluster, a bunch of wishweeds.

To blow the seeds from a wishweed takes more breath than dandelions. The kind of breath seven-year-olds have in their lungs. On autumn days, when I walk along the trail, sometimes wishes come spinning through the sky. I always try to catch them, but they float out of reach. Feathers from a plucked baby bird. Or they look like jellyfish. Like this whole time, I've been walking on the floor of some undisturbed ocean.

And We Spin Like Records
(and We Climb Like Trees)

IN THE MORNING, before I open my eyes, I imagine I live in a warm climate, I rent a rooftop room, there's no ceiling above me, only blue sky. But then I open my eyes, and I'm here, and I'm in Canada, and it's December again, freezing cold. Outside it's grey, but I have a map of South America tacked onto my wall. I look out my window, and if the sun is out, I let it hit my body, and for a moment I think the world might be a pretty okay place to figure out how to live, if I can exist in this apartment and have a map on my wall and have an imagination that can take me to far-off places this early in the morning.

There are a lot of windows in my apartment, which makes it almost as good as living on a rooftop, even if it's not all that big. So I walk over to my little kitchen area, grind some coffee, think some thoughts. And snow starts coming down, and it looks really nice, and I feel at peace for once. I sit at the table, I open my computer, and I scroll through my Facebook feed, and it turns out that in Connecticut there was a school shooting today.

Everyone's posting about it. At least eighteen people are dead, and more are in hospital. The kids that died are six or seven years old. I read article after article about it, but I can't stop repeating the story. Then I make some more coffee, and then I look out the window again. I think to myself, "You must be changed by this news, Kat, you must be." But outside it's still December. And I'm still in Toronto. And I still feel strangely at peace today, or maybe it's numbness, I don't know.

I started climbing things the day I realized my mom was never coming back. I don't really remember her too much – her dark hair, her eyes – I was only three when she left, and Dad didn't keep any pictures. She was from South America, I know that much. Maybe she ran off to discover her roots, to get away from my pasty-faced pops who is only interested in talking about records and bands from the 90s anyway. So I feel like I thought she'd come back until I was around five, which is pretty young to have an epiphany, but I swear I did. One day, I got home from school, and my dad wasn't there. I didn't know where he was. And I realized my mom'd never be there when I got home from school, and so I went into the backyard and I climbed a tree, and I just kept climbing until I got all the way to the top and I could see the roof of my house from there. I wished there were more branches, so I could climb up into cloud and sky. Maybe I could jump onto the back of a bird, and it would take me to where my mom was. But I didn't. I just stayed sitting in the tree, even after I had to pee so bad it killed my whole torso with cramps. Even after I heard my dad running around shouting, "Katrina! Katrina! Katrina!" and then finally just "KAY! KAY!" as if the short form would be what magically summoned me. He ran around the front of the house, and I climbed down. I snuck in the back door and peed in the basement washroom. Then I sat in a big chair in the living room with a book. My dad walked into the house, one hand pressed against the bridge of his nose.

"Hi Dad," I said.

"Kat! I've been looking for you everywhere."

"I've been sitting right here."

I don't know if he knew I was hiding, or understood why sometimes I needed to hide, or sometimes my energy or imagination got out of control. It was just easier not to talk about it. To grow up climbing, to grow talking about music instead of feelings, yeah, that's the way we did it. Later, when I was in high school, we moved to the city, and Dad opened the record store, and I found other things to climb.

I meet Paul at the rock-climbing gym, and we change into our shoes and grab chalk bags and dunk our hands into the white mess and rub them together as if we're trying to get warm. We decide to just boulder today instead of belaying, which means we aren't using harnesses and aren't going up too high. We try to go during the day when we both have a gap in our schedules - Paul doesn't have a class and I'm not working at Dad's store - so then we have the gym free of groups. But when I'm almost at the top, vaulting myself over the edge of the upper level, I see them. A parade of kids in miniscule rock-climbing shoes, T-shirts, and tank tops that say Team Boulderz. It must be almost 4 p.m. They high-five the instructors. I haul myself over the top of the wall. As I walk down the back steps, the kids have already started to use the low climbing wall to practice sideways movements. Their small bodies hug the wall, their legs criss-crossing, arms pulling themselves along. With them plastered up against the wall, it's so easy for me to imagine someone entering with a rifle; they are the right age, the ages of the kids that died today. Bullets ripping their tank tops and bodies to shreds.

I find Paul starting to climb the wall that's really low, built on an extreme angle, so it's like crawling across the ceiling like an ant. "Yo, I need to get out of here," I tell him. He lets himself fall to the mat, only a foot below. He lies flat on his back.

"You tired?"

"My hands ache."

"Okay, let's go. There are kids here anyway."

I feel like they are watching me as I pull out my hair tie and let my dark hair fall down to my shoulders. I unvelcro my climbing shoes. I wish I could take all of them and throw them into the air where they could land on the back of large birds that would take them far away from places where people kill each other. I want to explain to them that they aren't getting anywhere climbing, it's like running on a treadmill. You just go up, and then you go down. It's not like going up and up and up forever. I used to think when I was their age, I could fill my lungs with air by breathing in really deep and holding my breath, two balloons in my chest, and I would float away. Paul sees me looking over at the kids and laughs. "I know, eh? Uh, kids. How disgusting."

"I wouldn't mind having one, one day." He looks at me like he's surprised by this Katrina in front of him revealing tenderness towards these small animals. The rock-climbing kids, there was such precision in their movements. I could never be that precise even if I climbed every day. "Did you hear about all the kids that died?"

We walk outside, winter coats making our bodies puffy and lame. "Yeah, fucked up. I think I might have to get drunk tonight."

"But it's like, don't you think it's weird to look around and have everything the same?"

"I guess so, but people die all the time."

"They were shot."

"People also get shot all the time."

We cut through Bloor West, down Sterling, walk past the art lofts there. "I'm going to get a studio here," I tell him, more just to change the subject, before we both get too blue.

"It's so depressing."

"No it's not. There's something exciting about it all, like a dirty discarded canvas, you know?"

After you climb enough, eventually everything looks like a surface you can climb. Paul wants to learn how to parkour, but neither of us have ever been good at gymnastics, only climbing. On Sterling, we grab onto fire escapes and climb up the outside, using the railing as footholds, jump from landings to the ground. "I was researching parkour when I got bored with writing my Post-colonial Lit paper last night," Paul tells me. "Did you know it's also known as 'The Art of Displacement'?"

Sometimes when Paul talks, I feel like a big idiot because I'm not going to school and have a hard time being as articulate as he is. But then again I'm barely twenty-one and he's almost thirty. As I leap from the fire escape to the asphalt underneath me, the art of displacement starts to make sense, the air hits my body, and I feel like I'm a big bird that would be able to carry kids and whoever else needed to get away. I can fly to South America or anywhere in the country; my body is out of place.

"It's about using spaces differently," Paul says.

"We'll use this whole city!"

It's dangerous, what we're doing, especially since most the surfaces we're grabbing are covered with ice and snow and we're wearing gloves instead of going at it with our bare hands. But eventually we get up high enough that we're able to jump from the fire escape to the roof beside us. The sun is out, warming up my body, and it feels good. It feels like living on a roof in South America. I stare directly into the sun, like they tell you not to do when you're a kid. If you look at it for long enough, a blotch starts to grow in the middle like it's a dark bullet hole piercing through the sun, or like the sun is a record, spinning in the sky.

Some music my dad's really into, I never really understood. The moody way the singers moaned and the lyrics coming out about not knowing where you're going or who you are or what you want. But the more I climb, the more I understand. In the mornings when I daydream, I understand. When I think about my mom. I really understand what it all means - I mean I understand what the whole world means, where I'm going, and who I am, and maybe even a bit of what I want - when I listen to this crazy jazz band that my friend is in, or listen to any crazy instrumental music really, and I put my head down and I dance almost too wildly and the colours of the stage lights blend as I fling my head around and the world becomes blurs of reds and yellows and sometimes blues and for a moment, I think maybe all the band is playing is accidentals, that life is only accidentals, and then I dance harder and sometimes I almost fall down.

Paul and I don't say anything up on top of the roof. Sometimes we're able to have these moments of silence, and this is one of them. I find that, even though sometimes I get into what my dad calls a "babble mood" where I don't stop talking, my body's what really doesn't shut up and I can go a whole day or hang out with a friend and only have my body do the talking. Paul seems perceptive of all of this. I fill up my lungs with air like when I was kid to see if I will float, but I stay on the roof and I'm okay with that.

Voices of two men drift up to us. They sound angry and soon they are yelling down there on the ground. Paul must know something I don't because he grabs my arm and pulls me down beside this weird metal chimney thing, and we hide. He puts a finger to his lips. I can tell that they are on the ground below the building. The men would never see us up here. I move over to the edge of the roof and peer down. There're two guys down there, both really skinny. One's short, and the other is taller. The taller one yells at the shorter one. The short guy is pleading, it sounds like. Both of them have their hands in their coat pockets, chilled by the cold.

Paul doesn't come over to where I watch. He's got his eyes closed and is pressed to the side of the chimney. He's unaware of me, somewhere deep within himself. My dad does that too. When something comes on the TV that bums him out, he closes his eyes for a moment and breathes out his mouth, slow and calm. Then he opens his eyes and is himself again.

On the ground below, the tall man lunges for the short man and grabs his coat. He shakes him. I'm still seeing a dark spot in my vision from staring at the sun too long, and it spreads out right over where the two men are. The short man gropes for something in his back pocket. The tall man is faster.

The sound of a shot goes off, and the short man collapses. The tall man runs, and how fast he can run, he runs and he runs and he runs. The dark spot in my vision, right over the man on the ground, starts to go away, but there's still a dark spot there. It's not from my blotchy vision anymore. It's from blood.

"Kat, we have to go," says Paul. "Let's go."

We hop down fire escape stairs, using them the way they were intended, to escape, to escape. The city's not our playground anymore. We run all the way down Dundas and then down Roncesvalles and then we run up the stairs to my apartment and drink glasses of water. We don't even look at each other or hug like you might expect friends would do. My skin doesn't feel quite right. Paul calls the cops and explains why we fled and tells them where the body is, and we'll both go in for questioning. I look out the windows in my kitchen, and I think to myself, "You must be changed by all this, Kat, you must be." It starts snowing again. I don't know if it'll ever stop.

People are dying and being born all over the world, and some of those people who are born will one day be shot. If for every person, there was a big bird that could take them away, far away from the places all their pain and confusion are, from places where they don't know what they want, the sky would be crowded with wings. Flying up in the sky would be like walking onto a crowded streetcar, and everyone would want the same thing, to go to the same places. There aren't enough rooftop apartments in South America for everyone. Paul's taking care of everything, and my hands won't stop shaking. The sun's still up in the sky, some big bird's eye.

Below the Spoon-Tree

ONE STORY PAUL LIKED to tell took place in a field of sumac trees. He was eleven and his sister was nineteen. She'd come home different. Something had happened to her at university and made her wild. As Paul told this story to Jayme, he traced her spine with his fingertips - this was when they first got together, although sometimes she didn't answer his calls. "Something was wrong with her. She went walking on her own, so I followed her into the field of sumacs that bordered our property. I could barely see her, she cut so quickly into the grove. I saw that she'd broken a branch from a tree and was swinging at the bright red berries that clustered at the tops of the trees. I thought it was a game until I saw how angry she was. It was when I got closer that she swung at me. I picked up the nearest branch and swung back at her, and we fought like that for what felt like an hour. She finally got a hit in at me - gave me this scar." Paul peeled away his hair to show a line above his eyebrow. "Anyway, we never knew what made her so angry. Maybe just temporary madness."

That story was almost true. Not like lying to Jayme about quitting smoking, not like the fake resumés and the school that didn't quite exist. Paul was never important enough to look up anyway. He liked building, weaving, threading story into story, constructing something big and wondrous, but still mundane and miniscule.

The voices scattered over Paul's backyard from next door, and he flicked his cigarette into the bushes. The sound lured Paul to his neighbour's yard. Children ran from tree to tree, covered in twisted strands of white outdoor lights. Men held beer by a barbeque, while women sat at a row of picnic tables, some with babies teetering on their laps. Voices gathered menacingly, a dark swarm of birds. A stream of children ducked around Paul's legs and into the amalgam of adults, who didn't notice them. The kids howled savagely as they ran, stabbing in front of them with sticks broken from the trees. Paul grabbed a beer and walked to the grill.

A man paced by the bucket of beers, not talking to anyone, apart from the crowd, like Paul. He told Paul his name was Raj once Paul got him talking. Parties like this made him nervous. He plunged his hand into the beer bucket and fished through ice water for two more cans. Raj wasn't even finished his first. They talked about their new babies, Paul's fictitious and left at home. "Liam's right over there," Raj said and pointed to an abandoned stroller tucked beside a tree trunk. A mass moved under a blanket, and Paul tried to make out features. From where he stood, it was just a lump; he couldn't even see limbs. "How do you know Gary?"

"We worked together a while back."

"At the bank?"

"Yeah, we never got too close. I transferred to another branch soon after he started."

Raj looked over at one woman, slightly apart from the others, although still engaged in the conversation, in charge of the conversation. "That's my wife. She'll like you." Raj and Paul broke from the men and walked towards the women.

The woman had dark slicked-back hair. Her eyes were far apart. "This is Melanie." The name was much too delicate for her stern, cruel mouth, which curved into a smile as she caught sight of Paul. The other men were all in button-up plaid shirts, ironed khakis or dress pants. Paul was still dressed in a white T-shirt, wearing thin at the collar, blue jeans. His hair wasn't styled like these men, even their beards manicured by stylists, guided by magazines and their wives. She knew Paul was an imposter, he could see it in her eyes.

"Nice to meet you, Paul," Melanie said, shaking his hand. Raj excused himself to go check the baby, and it was Paul who glanced fretfully after him instead of Melanie. "Don't worry about Raj, he always has to keep moving," she said and flicked out her arm in a gesture that was very much like Raj.

"He told me about your baby. And that you like parties."

"Raj will reveal anything if you talk to him for long enough. That's why I have to keep my personal business under lock and key."

Raj spoke to a man who Paul assumed was Gary, and Gary looked over at Paul and shrugged. He couldn't remember if he'd met Paul, but there could've been a Paul, he knew many Pauls, his Facebook and LinkedIn were full of them. Raj waved at Paul, and Paul waved back at both of them, grateful they chose to stay on the other side of the backyard. "What personal business?" he asked her.

Melanie shook her head, reaching for the cigarette that Paul had freshly lit.

One story Paul liked to tell took place in a supermarket. He was three and his mother let go of his hand for just a minute, and he wandered along the aisles looking for chocolate until he was horribly lost. Paul was aware of his smallness and knew he needed help finding his mother. He ran to the produce section, tomatoes and stacks of broccoli in bins above his head. He could see his mother's back over by the celery, so far away. Why wasn't she searching for him too? He called out to her, and beside him, a produce worker shoved an empty crate underneath the stand. Paul heard chirping and peaked past crates and bins. In an empty box was a nest of birds, shrieking for their mother, their beaks gaping open. Paul always told this as his first real memory.

Paul moved closer to Melanie. He could smell her perfume

or a product in her hair. He wanted to know what it was
so he could wash his bed sheets in it. She had interesting eyes, green-pepper eyes, which studied the children's
brutal game, disinterested, as if she were their overlord.
"What are they doing?"

"It's a game we used to play too, back when we were
young, remember. It's called Manhunt."

"Manhunt?" He'd played in the woods; he'd hidden
behind bushes, while his friends had searched him out.
There had been no sharpened sticks, no warrior cries.

Two kids pushed past Paul, and he finally caught what
they were howling. "Kill the intruder! Kill the intruder!"
Another child slammed into Paul's legs then spun away
as if he hadn't hit anything, as if Paul wasn't even there.
Everyone became intoxicated and the night grew darker.
The women and men started to speak to each other. It
started to become unclear who belonged to who – because
these women and men did seem to *belong* to each other in
a different sort of way than Paul and Jayme. It even started
to become unclear who was who, faces interchangeable.

Someone familiar was in the group of bodies. Paul recognized the messy hair, the T-shirt with the worn collar,
the face covered in stubble and his sharp grin. Paul mo-
mentarily thought a wall of mirrors had been set up in the
middle of the party, or that rather than staring into the
crowd he was looking into the depths of a reflective pool
as his own face shimmered back at him. The figure pushed
through the crowd like the children, knocking people
aside who did not turn to watch where he was running.

He scaled the fence and dropped into Paul's backyard. The wooden fence was much too tall to climb. Paul wanted to follow the man, but he found himself unable to move from Melanie and his curiosity soon fell away as swiftly as the figure who'd disappeared from the crowd.

"You remind me of a boy I knew." Melanie reached out and touched the back of Paul's neck where his shaggy hair stopped. Her hand was cool, and for a moment, it calmed him. She slid her fingers up into his hair and gripped it gently, as if grabbing the loose scruff of a cat before dipping it into the water where it would be drowned. "His name was Paul too, but he died in a house fire. We were all very sad. They played music over the loudspeakers for him all day. That's what I remember about him the most, sitting in my classroom, staring at the green chalkboard, listening to the music for poor Paul."

"You can get right the fuck off me," he said, and her grip in his hair tightened. Her mouth curved upwards in that annoying expression, which he could not distinguish as smirk or smile.

"Stop now," she said, her face coming closer. "Raj wouldn't mind, if that's what you're worried about. He wouldn't even know." Paul never did the right thing. Usually he didn't even know what it was. He wanted to kiss her even as he thought instead of kissing him, she might gulp him up. But he liked Raj, and Raj seemed to like him. The two of them probably wouldn't even see each other ever again, but he knew the right thing and that's what mattered.

"I said, 'Get the fuck off me.'" Paul seized the hand tangled in his hair, pulled it out, and tossed it back at her. "You're a liar and prick," she said. "Everyone knows you aren't meant to be here. I bet your name isn't even Paul." She turned back to the group of women, away from him.

Paul stayed at her side, but she didn't face him again. She resumed the conversation with the women. Her words hovered around him, but, confronted with her back, he wondered if the exchange had even taken place. Gary and Raj studied him from across the backyard. Raj's face, which Paul had come to expect to always be drawn in nervous smile, was severe. Gary pointed at Paul and whispered to Raj. Paul cut through the crowd of people, slowly clustering around him, to the grove of trees studded with tiny lights.

From a tree dangled wooden spoons, knocking against each other, rattling like hollow wind chimes. Children had decorated them to look like themselves or one of their closest friends. Where the spoons curved inwards, they drew wavering smiles and dots for eyes. Yarn made hair. Some of the spoons had pipe-cleaner arms, but most were armless, heads attached to marker-coloured sticks covered in twisted ribbon. Slip-knot loops held the necks to yarn that connected them to the tree. The spoons twisted on their strings. He reached for one and turned it around. A name was written in unsure letters on the spoon's back. Anna, written with backwards Ns. He turned the next one around, expecting a Bryan or a Jim or an Alex, even a Kate, a little girl with short hair and a frown, blue and green ribbon choking her body. But the name on the back in crooked lettering was Paul. He tore the spoon from the tree.

Once Jayme leaned on his body on his front porch and told him all about her lousy childhood. "Join the club," Paul said and threw his cigarette into the street.

"Was it bad, Paul?" Snow was falling down.

"Yeah, I guess. Everyone has a bit of a rotten time."

He told her about one time when he ran away because his "uncle" hit his mom. He didn't bring anything except some T-shirts with him. The sun was setting, and he ran towards the next town. He wasn't crying because boys weren't supposed to do that once they were nine, and the sun set, and it was dark. He slept in a field, and he dreamt of his sister trapped in a vague, suffocating blackness. She was throwing something at his head and he was falling down against the ground, grass in his mouth. In the morning, he walked all the way to his grandparents' house - fifteen kilometres - and they let him stay over for the summer. When he got back home for school in the fall, the uncle was gone, and his sister wouldn't speak to him.

"Sounds like something from a book," Jayme said.

"Yeah, well . . ." But that story was the closest. Take away some kilometres, add a few years to his age, maybe the real Paul never returned. All of it filled him with a bitterness hard to contain.

That night, he and Jayme had sex; she bounced on top of him, and he sat straight up and reached out and touched the inside arches of both her feet. His fingers stayed there for only a second before he lay back down, but she told him in the morning that she was charmed by the tenderness. It was the spot on her feet that hurt all the time.

Below the spoon-tree was a stroller. Liam stared at Paul with green-pepper eyes, too far apart. His mouth already tried to simultaneously seduce and humiliate Paul. He couldn't see Melanie through the crowd of distracted people, and no one was watching the baby. Paul picked the blanket off the baby and dropped it to the ground. Let it get a chill this cold summer night.

The baby's hair, so jet black, made it look like Raj. If only it weren't for the eyes. Another breeze clicked the spoons together. The baby's eyes, Melanie's eyes, followed him. "What?" Paul shouted at the baby. "What do you want?" And it smiled. It waved a little fat arm in the air in a way that was like Raj, like Melanie mocking Raj.

His smack was louder than he'd expected. Then howling. The arm bent off to the side, and Paul looked down as the green eyes fused shut with pain. One of the children, her blond hair wild, gripping sharpened stick, stood below the spoon-tree. She would remember what he looked like. She knew who he was.

Paul ran like another summer night when he knew he needed to get away and become someone different. He ran out of the backyard, pushing past bodies and crooked arms that reached for him. He ran into the street and up into his home, because he couldn't call Jayme, she wouldn't answer, and he had nowhere to hide, there was nowhere to go.

Paul looked out the window of his apartment, and the sirens built to an orchestra pitch, the wail of a beaten child. Behind their shrillness were voices in a swarm, buzzing and twisting in childish, unsynchronized dissonance: Kill the intruder! Kill the intruder! Paul crouched below the window, the chants lashing at the walls of his room, scattering along the floor, accumulating by his feet. Outside, a car pulled into the driveway.

The Letters

WE'D BARELY BEEN married a year when I found the letters. We'd moved into our first home, and the responsibility of unpacking fell on me since Julia's father was incredibly ill. Only after Julia died of the same stomach cancer that took her father could I even begin to recollect some of those early times. Standing on the front porch of our house, watching the sun go down, casting its gold all over our front lawn, groundcover and trimmed weeds instead of grass, our soil too sandy.

The items I pulled from the boxes spoke of our new life together. We got married in 1960, but had already done the scandalous by living together for six months at college, away from our parent's judgment. We might have kept living in that scummy student apartment if it hadn't been for her father getting sick, snapping a couple of twenty-year-olds out of our period of experimentation with non-tradition, drugs, and music and into a settled life that we both found rich and satisfying, even if it didn't have the excitement of those early days. It took another six months to find the perfect house to buy, and by then, her father was in the hospital, waiting. I lined the things he'd given us up on the kitchen table after I unpacked them. I should've just put them away.

The table had been passed down from my parents, a beautiful mahogany scarred from my mother's first days as a housewife before she knew the damage heat could do. The box was also mahogany, another part of us that matched, long with a bronze latch. I opened it. I expected a set of carving knives or a wedding present I'd forgotten. Inside were a bundle of letters. To Julia from a Paul Wilder. I looked at the name again. I walked to my bookshelf, books unpacked but unalphabetized. A thick literary war novel by Paul Wilder. It'd been a blockbuster, everyone talked about it, but Julia had never even mentioned it in her list of favourite books. The novel was mine.

I still regret doing what I did. Fifty-five years of marriage taught me that even in the most open marriages, people are allowed their secrets. Or maybe not secrets, but privacy. Those letters were hers. They were private, but I undid the twine that bundled them together and began to read.

Their love affair began when Julia was sixteen. At thirty-two, he was double her age and had already written his superstar book. She was in a little high school play with one of his friend's younger sisters. Maybe it was the sister that made her seem approachable, but that's not the way

Julia told it. I admit to seeing a picture of Julia at sixteen or fifteen, one of those posed school photos, and letting out a whistle and giving her a wink, and I regret it now. I regretted it then as she told me.

He found her address from his friend's sister and started sending her letters, and when she saw who the letters were from, she was filled with the flattery of it. Finally she was being noticed. Already in the first letter, he was so familiar in a way I'd never be.

I can tell from seeing you on stage you understand this world. I've never seen someone deliver her lines like you! Being around each other, we'd feel at peace, that ultimate understanding. I know you felt it too.

So bold and romantic. I feel I'm romantic, or I was back then, I was with her. I prioritized her in a way that felt like romance. But with Wilder, it was something different. Grand gestures and impulsiveness, and since she was sixteen, she sunk right into it and started to plan running away. I read all the letters, spanning five months. The last one a farewell until they saw each other in person.

I spent four nauseous days without telling her. I listened when she called and often fell asleep to her voice. While I kept that secret, I craved her more. I needed her words, like I assumed she'd given him her words. I needed her voice more than I needed her body. I asked her the night before she called me from the hospital, asking me to come because he was dead, "Why didn't we ever write to each other?"

"Well, we saw each other every day in class, and when we wanted to talk, you were just a phone call or a short walk away."

"Do you wish we had?"

"Written letters? I don't know. I don't think I would change anything about what happened."

She was right, as she tended to be. We had our issues to figure out, especially in the beginning few months, but what emerged quite quickly was a breathless dedication to each other, which made me lighter. We were both so sure of each other.

Except I knew her well. Even before I found them, I always knew she was withholding something from me, and it was this that gave me a little shake as we kissed, not our spark, but the danger and thrill of knowing there was a mysterious infidelity.

Is withholding unfaithful? Are secrets an infidelity? That's what it felt like when I spread those letters in front of me, each one a little story she'd never told me. Imagine packing up at sixteen. I couldn't. At eighteen I'd gone off to college, but I still had long conversations on the telephone with my mother. It was she who I wrote letters to, not already entangled in some torrid love affair.

And the words he used! I'll never forget those words.

Your last response came just in time. I was feeling lonesome. The way you described your body tingling, even the bottoms of your feet as you read my letter, damn, I'm jealous of those feet. Attached to you. I bet even your feet are gorgeous.

She kept her socks on when we made love. Was it because of him? Was he the reason I only saw her completely naked when we took showers, or that time we found a creek on our drive home from Muskoka? Boiling hot from the drive, we cut down through the trees and pulled the clothes from each other, splashed in the water, made love on the bank even though I worried another passing traveller might pull over for a dip.

I know it's wrong that during the beginning I thought of her as mine, but that's what we told each other and that's what really caused the feeling of betrayal. Possession. That it wasn't there.

I drove two hours to the house her mother now lived in alone. I held a bouquet of white lilies, the flowers trite and insignificant, and I put them aside as soon as I saw Julia and her mother, wrapped each of them in my arms. We were all dressed in black, and I put my hand on the small of Julia's back and imagined my touch was something that burned. The casket was closed because he had wasted away - Julia said she'd barely recognized him at the end. Except for the eyes.

We spent two days there with her mother, who begged us, "Please eat this food. I never will," as neighbours brought more and more. I ate and didn't speak. I still didn't tell Julia what I'd found.

I worried there would never be a right time. Back at our new home, Julia raced from room to room, looking at how I'd set it all up. "Oh, such a lovely job!" she kept saying. "It's so wonderful." We went downstairs, and I handed her the box.

"I read . . ." Her look stopped me. The way she touched the letters, as if they were fragile, near dust.

"What do you want to know?" she asked. She didn't chastise me or criticize my prying.

"All of it," I said.

"It might take a while."

"I've missed you." It was the first time I said it. I wasn't expecting her to beam. "It can take all night." I grabbed a bottle of wine from the pantry, and we sat on the floor in front of our fireplace. We faced each other, cross-legged like kids, knees touching. I knew no matter what she told me, I'd forgive her. I was ready.

She described the awkward moment when she arrived to live with him, her first moment of feeling unsure. She looked at his grey hair, starting to come in at his temples. At least it wasn't thinning, she told herself. "Where am I going to sleep?"

"You're really the sweetest thing. You can just sleep in my bed."

For the past five months, she'd gone to bed every night going over his words. She knew that, like he told her, they were perfect for each other, that their bond was one of a kind. She wasn't sure if she was ready, but rather than reason that if she wasn't ready someone kind would wait for her to be ready, older, anything that she still needed to become, she decided that sometimes you weren't ready when you met the right person. Fate works in mysterious ways. It's either you grow up or lose that person. She decided to grow up.

It wasn't what she thought it would be, but she didn't really know that was unnatural at the time. That he pressed his hands over her mouth, and for a moment she was afraid she would suffocate.

He released her just in time, and then he grabbed for her hair, and she said, "He, well, he kind of forced me, but I didn't really know better. He pushed my head down, you know, because he said he didn't want children, and this way we wouldn't have any children. I wondered if women were supposed to like it. If that was his love. I felt totally swallowed up, and I convinced myself I was ravenous for that feeling.

"I stopped being able to think. I forgot who my parents were. I don't know how to properly explain it. After a while when I looked in the mirror, and I was alone, I didn't see myself, just that he wasn't with me. He told me soulmates were like two pieces of a puzzle and there were no other pieces, there was only us. Other than the times I went shopping, there was only us. The house was surrounded by forest on each side, and I spent the days cooking and cleaning for him, although I missed school and learning. He kept telling me he was going to teach me all about writing, that I would write like him, I would be a star. I didn't even know if I wanted to write; I had wanted to act before he swept me away, but I trusted him. For no reason except for the fact he was now everything.

"One day I was late with dinner. I'd gone for our shopping and left him writing, and then I'd seen a nice dress in a store window. He gave me a little extra spending money, and I thought that he'd think I was beautiful in that dress, red with a plunging neckline and no back. So I bought it, and when he went out for his afternoon walk, I got dressed and put on some lipstick I'd stolen from my mother before I'd left home. I looked at myself in the mirror, and I could see myself. I was all grown up, already, and it'd only been a couple of months. I used water on my lashes to make them cling together. Then I got started on dinner. He liked to have it ready when he came in, and it was still cooking when he got back from his walk. I presented myself.

"'Where's dinner?' he asked. He never kissed me hello or goodbye. He told me real couples didn't kiss each other. They just did what we did and had some class in the waking hours. I wanted to have class, but I also wanted to be kissed.

"'It's coming,' I said. 'It just took me a while to get ready.' He hadn't noticed the dress or me yet, and then he focused. I gave him my best movie-star grin, and his whole face got dark and he slapped me. We were lucky we didn't have any neighbours because I don't think I'd ever howled like that.

"'You look like some tramp,' he said and left. I finished making dinner, and then I wiped off the lipstick, and I changed back into my grey skirt, the one I used to wear to school. We ate quietly and quickly, and then he took me

130

to the bedroom, and he hit me there too, during. He held me afterwards, and he told me how much he loved me. How it'd hurt him to see me like that, to think of me buying a dress like that. I promised to return it the next day. He loved my innocence and purity, he said, and he didn't want me to throw it away so easily. Finally, wrapped in him, I felt comforted.

"He hit me a few times, but it was always as a punishment. He never beat me up or used a closed fist. But it wasn't right."

"How did you get out? How did you know to leave?"

"Well, he broke up with me eventually. He met someone younger. I was turning seventeen. I already was getting too old. I couldn't do anything right. Sometimes I cried, and he hated that. I laughed too hard, and he hated that. It just wasn't a good match. He told me to call my mother, and I remembered her. She came to pick me up, and she was so glad to see me. She forgot to be humiliated by it all. And you know my dad, he was like you. He hugged me and gave me a kiss on my forehead like I was five years old. We just pretended it never happened."

"Except you kept the letters."

"Just put it away somewhere deep in your brain. That's what I did. Just forget it." And I did, I suppose. I forgot it for fifty-five years, but after she died, instead of dwelling on the time lost, yearning for the time that we'd never get back, feeling the good times, regretting the bad times, I ended up obsessing over a life that didn't involve me. Maybe it's because she was my first and last and will only ever be my one. While it was happening, it was easy to get caught up in our love as it evolved, but I was haunted by memories that weren't even mine.

"Just forget about it. I did."

But did she? Or did the ten months with him still follow her? The letters and seduction, the coercion and early romance. I wasn't the first man she'd lived with. But I was the only man she'd married and that had to count for something. It surfaced in various ways. Without children, our lovemaking was only for enjoyment and sometimes I made the comparison. I once asked her, under the sheets, if she wished I were more aggressive. She'd giggled and said, "Oh no!" but I wondered if every intimacy contained a lie. Sometimes when we were in the kitchen, she'd stare out the window, daydreaming, and I knew she was thinking of her previous life.

It was a few nights after her funeral, after waking up in the blackness of our bedroom and forgetting she'd gotten sick and died or that we'd even aged, that I swore she left me to find him again. The kind of grief you couldn't weep for, that loss. I rolled over and pressed my face to my pillow, trying to smell her smell, which had been gone for a while now . . . She'd been in the hospital, but in that moment, she'd left me sleeping, alone. When I woke up, I knew it wasn't true, but there was something dark and small and bitter that was starting to grow from all of those pieces over the years.

The first thing I did was burn his novel. I stacked logs

and I lit a match and I threw the book in, and then it was gone. Pages that crisped and then vanished into ash. It eased me for a moment, the sun had not completely risen, and I made coffee and began my morning routine. Without her. Where was Paul Wilder? I'd buy all his books from a bookstore and burn those too. Spend Julia's life insurance on burning his books, setting fire to his words. With the funeral paid for, I didn't need the money, I had my pension and no one to leave anything to, when I died, as I would. I hoped soon to erase these mornings and the nights of forgetting. I went up to the attic on a hunch, to where she kept her old school diaries and address books. I found the oldest address book and looked up Wilder, and then I looked up Paul, and there it was in her teen girl's cursive. The hunch was still there, as were several more address books from later years. She saved everything. This is why she told me she had kept the letters. So that she'd never forget her past. Under each P, his address, years and years into our marriage, until she stopped using address books and used a cellphone, such a quick learner, not like me. How many more letters were there? Did she send birthday cards, Christmas cards, complaints about me? I threw one of the address books into an old leather backpack that I'd had for years, along with a map. See, I'd always been faithful to both things and people.

The mailbox had his last name on it, painted in beautiful bold letters right on the side in red. I imagined them peeling off, one by one, fluttering to the ground at my feet. He was dead. Of course. She was dead. My Julia. The bat I'd brought was one I'd bought in my twenties. The guys at work were starting a softball league, but I was never a really good slugger. *Too gentle,* Julia had said. I think gentle's not from a lack of strength, but from a lack of will to be a brute, and out there on the road, my seventies fell from me and those years with Julia, I was seventeen again, and I was a brute, I had that will, the bat in my hands and crushing the mailbox and those taunting letters. The bat was splintering, too old, but God knows age is just a number, an arrangement of letters and characteristics, and it can all collapse in an instant.

What was I left with? A bat in pieces and a wife in the ground. The tin mailbox split and dented. Crushed. All of me crushed. When I went home, I searched for those letters, but couldn't find them. I imagined her buried with them, tucked up against her skin under the lace of a bra. I imagined her buried, not with her body waned away, but with the full voluptuousness of twenty, first married, telling me the story in front of the fireplace and still somehow withholding. Despite that moment of vulnerability, the spark of secrecy in her eye. I was not wrong when I was young, pressing my mouth to her, against the heat of the fire, in thinking we were destined for each other. Destiny isn't always a good thing; we're all destined for someone or something or another, and sometimes it's for a life with someone who loves you less.

Degenerate

1.

WIND WAS WHAT WORKED its mischievous ways on Toronto, on the wild of the city. Caught leaves and threw them against fences, brought the frost with it. It was cold with the sun and without the sun. If you listened hard enough, wind was what told the stories about everything, pushed people around like they were toys, models made of clay. This must be why he kept going by her house even though all his friends said he shouldn't, why three girls huddled into bed together, their phones going off in unison as degenerate after degenerate after degenerate called and texted, wind pushing hard against the windows and apartment door, promising the ice would come. The real frost had not even begun.

The west end of Toronto was a collection of villages pillaged by degenerates and wind. Paulina snuggled into the sleeping back of her degenerate in Roncesvalles Village, where she counted his pills and snapped strands of her untameable golden hair, her eyes always distracted, knotted scars on the back of her hands. Wild, until she broke into her wide, awkward smile, as she always did, especially when there was something she didn't want to say. Kayla danced in an apartment above a candy shop in Little Italy until her legs couldn't anymore, always needed another party to go to, more people to talk to, needed to dance The Restlessness out, always called Paul and Stef, "Come over, come over, I'm bored! There's gotta be something better to do!" In The Junction, Stef watched Derek give her six-year-old Wynn her own deck of cards and teach her Snap, while she marked papers at the kitchen table. Her dark hair always pulled back so it wouldn't get in her face as she ran, always late, to work, to Paul's, to Kayla's, to Wynn, to Derek, to work, to The Cave where everyone knew they'd never be able to drink enough.

The summer before Kayla met her degenerate, Paul convinced herself she was deeply in love. She and her degenerate both were out of money, as were most of their friends, and they spent the summer walking along the lakeshore. Sometimes he'd stare at the water, and sometimes she was able to convince him to hold her hand, although most times she wrapped her body around him and promised him nothing bad was ever going to happen to him, she wouldn't let anything bad happen to him, she would always be there for him. When he looked out at the water, sometimes he came up with things to say to her, or to the water, or maybe to the world in general.

While Paul had always felt like she couldn't count on anything, she counted on his words, even when they didn't make much sense. The sun warmed her skin, it felt like the promises she'd made to him. Nothing bad, nothing bad, nothing bad will ever happen. She only believed this when she said it to him.

Briefly on the beach, they separated. He sang to the sky and the waves, and she hurled stone after stone at the water, listening to the hard plunks. He walked up to her, far enough back that she didn't realize, but close enough that he could watch her. The expression on her face. She kept flinging the stones, feeling the snap of her arm, the burning in her elbow. He didn't watch the stones as they broke through the lake's surface, only her. When she turned to him, she couldn't tell what he was thinking.

As they walked home, his mood changed. "The problem with you and all your friends - "

"They're your friends too."

" - you're all so shallow, so young, you haven't felt your death yet, you don't know what it'd be like to die, and you're all afraid. And angry. I see how scared you all are. I'm not afraid like that. I'd welcome death if it came for me."

"Don't say that," she said and tried to put her arm around him again, but he ducked into a convenience store and came out with a bag full of chocolate bars. He handed her one, and she appreciated his thoughtfulness.

She'd loved someone else once, sometimes she still loved him. She thought about him all the time. But he'd never let her take care of him. He'd never walked with her along the lake or needed her to remind him about his pills or talked to her enough even to complain about their friends.

Once they were home, and her degenerate was passed out on their bed, Paul took a hot shower that fogged up the bathroom windows. She stood naked in front of the mirror. She waited for the mirror to fog up too. She watched her face disappear under a veil of mist. She imagined that the fog was frost, clinging to the windows, even inside the apartment. The air felt like it'd rained. She ducked into the shower. The water beat against her face. Even then she knew what was going to happen. Every promise she had made to her degenerate by the lake had been a lie.

2.

Kayla found her degenerate last. At the beginning of September, when the days were still warm, she found herself lost at a party in an attic apartment, sharing a bill with a man who claimed he already loved her. "Whatever you got I want, babe," he said as she chatted away at him about what diseases you could get from sharing bills, and then danced from person to person having conversations, all while the degenerate rubbed his hand through his long black hair again and again, an open-mouthed smile with lips that hid his teeth, his eyes following her, dark eyes with a pupil that grew, getting darker.

She couldn't even remember giving him her number when he texted after the party. In conference with Stef and Paul, the three of them sitting cross-legged on her living room carpet, she decided not to text him back. Stef gave the same careful advice she always gave her about not being able to heal someone and not falling in love so easily, especially not with someone who sounded like bad news. As if because Stef lived with someone and had a well-paying job and a child, she was much more grown-up. As if her boyfriend, Derek, wasn't slipping down the slope of degeneration too. As perhaps they all were. The Restlessness lived in all three of them, Kayla knew, although in her, it was strongest.

Kayla blamed it on wind later . . . Or on Stef and Paul. That it was supposed to be just the three of them camping in Muskoka, but Stef and Paul each brought along their degenerates, and Kayla was lonely without someone to talk to after the couples had gone into their tents and wind made the night fierce and cold. Alone drinking whiskey under the stars by the fire the girls had built while the degenerates wandered in the woods, smoking pot. So she texted her degenerate, told him about the whiskey and the stars, the blanket that wasn't warm enough, the fire. She texted him about loneliness, and he texted, **ud never b lonly w me babe.** Already in love. Wind came through the trees, chilling Kayla even more.

The ice storm started back then really. Next weekend the weather turned, and by this time, Kayla was waking up beside her degenerate. His tongue tasted like cigarettes. His eyes were bloodshot with early morning and lack of sleep from staying up all night talking to Kayla about his past and then having sex and then talking more and then having more sex. "You're mine, right?" His eyes were barely open, and already he was asking.

Kayla said, "Of course. I thought it was obvious."

"You never know with girls."

"Well, what I say is what I mean, okay? That's how I am, and I care about you."

"You're mine."

"Yes, I'm yours."

It so quickly became October. In the last week, wind brought the first snow. Kayla watched it fall outside the window of the degenerate's house. She smoked by the window and the snow, it was the ashes of all her and the degenerate's cigarettes.

3.

"You've got a problem with rage," Paul's degenerate had told her that morning. It was the last day of November, and by now, something was always wrong with her. As she walked to Stef's, the grey November sky did fill her with tenderness that made her want to hurl her body at something. What did Kayla call it? The Restlessness. Trembling running through her like how all those branches on the trees were jolting, sharp and leafless against the sky. Wind pressed up against her back. She could never feel tender without also feeling angry. She regretted showing that side to her degenerate, telling him about the things she'd gone through, things she'd never even told Stef or Kayla. She only trusted him because he claimed to be sure about her. The Man She Used To Love/Still Loved was never sure.

"Sometimes I think we're at the end of it," she told Stef, once they were on the couch in the living room, watching Wynn use thin sheets of tracing paper to outline cartoon characters. Wynn held each one up and waited for a "Good!" She didn't tell Stef about her degenerate's criticisms, sure his meds were off. She wanted to tell Stef that most days she wished they actually were about to break up, she didn't know how much longer she could keep feeling this way.

"I think something's wrong with Derek too."

"What do you mean?"

"He's not home much anymore. He's always been really into being home, for Wynn. We always ate together. But now we barely see him. He comes home pretty late. I'm worried about it. He won't tell me what's wrong." Wynn was absorbed in her tracing, but Paul could tell she was listening.

"Do you think he's okay? Everyone goes through their times."

"There's definitely something."

Stef kept the house immaculate. On the wall, charts for tracking Wynn's growth, her behaviour, each night's dinner. Paul noticed how thin Stef was, the way her hands twisted over each other in her lap, one suffocating the other. Paul wrapped her in her arms. At least Paul's body was good at speaking.

In another part of the city, on this cold end of November day, Kayla was walking with her friend, Cam. He'd texted her that morning to get everyone out to The Cave that night, and they planned to spend the Saturday showing each other their favourite places in Roncesvalles.

"If it was warmer, I'd climb that tree," Kayla told him. The tree had a plaque on it saying that it was over one hundred years old. "Don't you think that'd be cool?"

Cam tested his shoe's grip against the base of the tree. "I could definitely climb it."

"I wouldn't be so sure about that." They walked away from the tree. "Aren't you going to try?" Cam once told her he'd never been in love, been with too many girls, and had a brief relationship which he slept with more girls to forget. His sister had been in an art collective with one of their friends a long time ago and eventually she'd moved away, as most people did eventually, leaving Cam, an engineer with a real day job, to fill her spot in their pack.

He dragged his hand along a railing in front of a school as they walked. His fingers picked up little bits of snow, which he formed into a tiny ball and chucked at Kayla. She screamed in protest, and he grabbed her into a hug, there on the street, and squinted his eyes at her, like a cat did when it was happy. "That used to be my high school," he said, separating from her. "I bet you were a popular girl in high school."

"I had a lot of friends, but I didn't go out with a lot of guys."

"That's surprising. You just seem like one of those people everyone would love." They started to walk up the steps to Cam's old high school, empty on a Saturday. More snow started to fall from the sky to replace the snow Cam had scraped from the railing.

She tried to catch his brown eyes again. She'd always had a thing for brown eyes, hadn't she? The degenerate had brown eyes, but they were different from Cam's, weren't alert in the same way. He pulled his toque down over his ears. And she remembered the degenerate, always pressing his face against hers. *You're mine.*

4.

All aching people sought out a bar called The Cave, too dark inside, candles tossed carelessly on the tables, casting a glow Kayla called chin-lit. No one knew who discovered the bar first. Maybe it was Stef, back when she was with Wynn's dad. Or Cam's sister, before she moved away. On Saturday nights, a band set up in front of the window. Stef, Kayla, and Paul and their pack of friends crammed into tables shoved against the wall of the narrow space. The bartender leaned on the counter, which wrapped around, taking too much space in the dark room. Above him, on the back wall, two glowing green lightbulbs flickered, the only artificial light in The Cave. When it was dark like this, people forgot that time passed, the band played song after growling song, while the bartender watched or chatted. The degenerates were always especially chatty with the bartender, seeing him as a real guy's guy, knowing if they chatted for long enough he'd pour them a drink on the house.

Wind howled down the street in front of The Cave, pushing Paul and her degenerate along to the bar, where they would meet Kayla and her degenerate, Stef, and a few others, and The Man She Used To Love/Still Loved. She never told anyone about him, hadn't even told the degenerate about the way he'd jerked her around, but Kayla and Stef saw the way some nights all her drinks collided in her until she was yelling like she was having a good time, the best time, but with tears running down her face. She either pretended they weren't there or wiped at them with the back of her hands, where the scars were.

The others were already there. The Man She Used To Love/Still Loved stood by himself at the bar's counter, sipping a rye and coke. He raised a hand in greeting to her degenerate, barely nodded at her. "Nice guy," her degenerate said, waving back. Paul crammed in along the bench at the table, crushed up against Kayla. The Man She Used to Love/Still Loved slid into the booth beside her. Kayla instantly decided this meant she should go outside for a cigarette, and the degenerates joined. The Man Paul Used To Love/Still Loved left Paul, Stef, and Cam inside, hoping to bum a smoke from the degenerates, who were always generous about sharing anything that would give them company, coughing in the cold.

"Where's Derek?" Paul asked Stef.

Stef checked her phone. "I'm not sure." She looked at The Cave's door, but it didn't open for Derek, and she didn't see him coming down the street through the front bar window. She bought two vodka shots and gave one to Paul. They tossed them back.

Kayla and The Man Paul Used To Love/Still Loved came inside, and Kayla made sure to sit between him and Paul. The Man She Used To Love/Still Loved decided this meant he didn't need to talk to anyone and stared into his drink. Periodically, he glared at Kayla. The degenerates drifted in and out, rolling joints on the bar table when the bartender's back was turned. Cam kicked at Kayla's feet under the table and rolled his eyes at her as the degenerates drifted outside again. Kayla smiled at him, and she and Paul watched their degenerates through the bar's front window where they smoked. Paul's degenerate laughing and telling a story to Kayla's, who blew out smoke and then leaned his head back so that all he could see was the sky and snow falling, catching in his lashes.

5.

In another part of the city, Derek left *her* apartment. He was staring at his phone, and he was drunk and he could still smell *her* on him and his lips felt raw from where *she*'d bit them. Back at *her* place, *she* always asked him to stay, but he thought about Wynn at home with the sitter, and then he looked at his new love and compared her to

147

Stef, tried to imagine a life without Stef and Wynn and then felt deeply embarrassed. As if he could ever have a life without them.

Derek saw Kayla's degenerate through the snow, blowing smoke straight up into the air. The degenerate waved at him and stuck the joint out. Derek took the joint from him, breathed in and then let the smoke drift away into wind. "I think I'm just going to go. It's so late. I didn't realize how late it was. I should get home to the sitter."

"Want me to grab Stef?" the degenerate asked.

"No, it's all right. Just tell her I came by after my work drinks. Tell her I went home for Wynn, okay?"

"Sure, man." The degenerate took back the joint and pulled Derek in for a hug, slapping him on the back. He took one last drag. "Here, bro, take the rest of this. For your walk."

"Thanks." Derek put the blunt between his lips and started to walk away.

"Oh, and hey, Derek!" the degenerate called.

"Yeah, man?"

"Make sure you take a shower, buddy."

Derek ran his hand through his hair and nodded. He waved at the degenerate and walked back down the street.

On the bar counter, Paul's degenerate rested his head, then raised it again, wanting to keep up his conversation with The Man Paul Used To Love/Still Loved and Kayla's degenerate. "I'm sorry, guys," he said. "I'm just so drunk."

"We're going home," Paul said and paid their tab.

"No!" Her degenerate put his head back on the bar.

"Seriously, we're going," she said. He sat back up and turned away from her, continuing his conversation with the guys. The Man She Used To Love/Still Loved didn't say anything, watched for her reaction. He, more than anyone, knew how angry Paul could get. She put on her coat, her toque.

She started to walk away, and her degenerate grabbed her arm, yanking her back over to him, pushing his face into hers. She winced and tore her arm away from him. "Where're you going?"

The Man She Used To Love/Still Loved had now stood and pulled on his own coat. "She wants to go home," he said. She gave her degenerate a twenty for a cab and dashed away to say bye to Kayla and Cam, the only other people left. The Man She Used To Love/Still Loved hovered nearby.

"Paul, don't go with him," Kayla whispered into her ear as she and Paul hugged. "You know how he is, and it will be a different story the next day. Okay? I know you don't want to talk about it, but I know something happened there, and it's just like, think about tomorrow. Don't think about tonight. Think about your guy! The guy you love!"

"Who says I love him?" Paul stepped away from Kayla and left The Cave, out into the street where the snow was starting to be whisked away by wind, The Man She Used To Love/Still Loved trailing behind her.

"I'm only walking this way because we live in the

same direction," he hollered after her as he followed her into the street.

"I don't care," Paul said. Wind caught her golden hair, trapped underneath her navy toque, pulled the ends with it, the strands creeping into her mouth. She let him catch up to her, and for a bit, they walked in silence.

"What's Kayla's deal anyway? She seemed to make a huge deal about me just walking with you. You never told her anything, did you? About us?"

"I never told anyone anything."

The Man Paul Used To Love/Still Loved was wearing Converse instead of proper shoes outside. They were now grey, even if they had started off being another colour, and the rubber was peeling away from the fabric, stained with salt. Paul knew he couldn't afford boots, and she knew his feet must be cold. She wished she could warm them. "So, with him," he said. He breathed a heavy sigh out and kept his eyes forward. "You would tell me if there was something wrong, right? Like if he needed a talking to, or if he was hurting you . . ."

"Why do you care?"

"Anything that happens to you is important to me."

Paul stopped walking. A streetcar rolled past, slowly creaking through the snow. "You never cared before."

"Look, Paulina, I'm trying to have a conversation. Just let me know if there's something wrong."

She couldn't look at The Man She Used to Love/Still Loved. She thought about the routine of her life, checking her degenerate's pills. Living with someone who was sick, forever, the sadness that brought. That she knew it was getting worse. That she was scared. All the things she'd never be able to tell The Man She Used To Love/ Still Loved. Never be able to tell anyone. "I will tell you if there's something wrong, sure."

She thought about what Kayla had said. Think about tomorrow. Think about her degenerate who she loved, didn't she, who she loved, but that tenderness was rising up in her that made her want to grit her teeth or hold his hand, whichever came first. He put his hand on her arm. She had always thought he had such beautiful hands, large and graceful, perfect hands, not like hers. "Paulina -"

"Don't touch me," she said.

"You know what, fine. I'm trying to help you, but you're drunk. You don't want my help."

"Just leave me alone."

"Whatever, Paulina, you're a loser," he said, but he was the one that turned and walked in the other direction, his shoulders brought up to the bottom of his ears.

"You're the one who's dangerous to me!" she shouted after him, but wind caught her words and blew them right back at her. This was the start of what would happen to Paul and her degenerate, wind was coming for him, even more than her, ready to blow his emotions about. The ice storm was coming. The Man She Used to Love/Still Loved's watching eyes had set something off, and wind would make it grow.

6.

Alone in her apartment, Kayla made a list of things she was learning about love, snatches of conversation from Stef and Paul, and also what she was experiencing with her degenerate too, what she was also experiencing with Cam.

If you want to help someone, that can become love.

If you are loved by someone, sometimes your own love goes away.

There is no love, there is only the way someone looks at you in the morning.

To love is to feel like you can understand all of someone with one look.

You can never understand anyone, even someone you love.

To love is to feel in a constant state of hope.

Hope is often misleading. To love is to be misled.

It was a dance that kept going, step this way, step back, she put on records in her house and closed her eyes and danced, and the degenerate was with her, or maybe it was Cam, who knew, who cared, who was holding her as she danced. She was entirely alone, but knew in another part of the city, the degenerate was existing, and Cam was existing, and Paul was existing with her degenerate, and Stef was existing with Derek, soon to be a degenerate too. Weren't they all beautiful, beautiful people, the way she was a beautiful, beautiful person? Who needed anyone, or loved anyone? Or everyone loved everyone, this coated them all. Even right now, her phone was lighting up with texts, so many wonderful, damaged people wanted to talk to her. Wind sang, *You know who you love, Kayla, and he needs you*, but today it didn't get through. It was just at the corners, trying to get in.

Paul was first. Beside her degenerate whose hand she held if he was feeling low, she had a dream about The Man She Used To Love/Still Loved. He walked beside her in a snowfall. The roads were slicked with ice. She was afraid they would both fall on the ice, but he held her up, hooking his arms underneath her shoulders. Braced this way, her back pressed against his chest, she was pushed along in front of him as he skidded along the ice. "I've got you," he said. "Don't worry, you're not going to fall." The sky was a brilliant grey, pulsing with the light of a sun hidden behind a blanket of cloud. "I'm sorry, for all those things I've said. We never know what to say to each other." She wanted to say something back to him, but she couldn't say anything, couldn't control her own feet, pushed forward, gliding along ice.

Awake, she stared at the face of her degenerate. When he had moved in, he'd seemed the antidote to The Man She Used To Love/Still Loved. To the degenerate, everything about her was fascinating and she was willing to take care of him, to be there beside him as he navigated his emotions that constantly betrayed him. She felt the degenerate made her almost altruistic, she hadn't done a selfish thing in the last year. Not even when The Man She Used To Love/Still Loved had walked her home and she'd wanted to let him rescue her, kiss her all over, and take her away from the degenerate, whose emotions also betrayed her. Maybe it was just that the degenerate saw all sides of her and that this was the real love, not that other thing she had felt for The Man She Used To Love/Still Loved, was still feeling. The degenerate opened his eyes.

"We're breaking up," she said.

"No," he said and closed his eyes again.

"You don't love me."

"I've just been tired. I've been exhausted. You know how I am." And then he fully woke, his eyes blinking at the ceiling. He rolled over on his side and stared at her. "What're you saying?" He reached out and grabbed her hand. "Don't you love me?" His hand closed around hers, crushing her fingers together, tighter and tighter. He knew the answer, somehow saw into her head, closed to others.

"You're hurting me. Don't do something you'll regret."

"Leave. I bet you're fucking someone." He released her hand. It throbbed, like the sky in her dream, a hidden light trying to break through.

Paul got out of bed, and she started crying. "I would never do that. I don't want to hurt you."

"Get out of here."

"My name's on the lease."

"You did this to yourself. Get out."

Paul grabbed her backpack and shoved her things in it. "I'm going to call your mom. She's got to know about this. Are you going to be all right?"

"Go!"

On the street, she called Kayla. She couldn't stop crying. "I broke up with him. I'm on my way to your place. He kicked me out."

"Are you all right?"

"Yes, I think I am."

It was easy to feel like this was another bad thing happening to her, the way bad things always happened to her. Since she'd moved to the city two years ago and even before. Sometimes on quiet nights when the three girls had nothing else to talk about, Paul heard the other girls describe the way the universe worked for them, the synchronicity, an imagined deity kindly interested in their well-being. Paul couldn't understand.

Wind was harsh that morning. She'd forgotten her hat and her hair whipped all around her, covered her eyes. She fled to the safety of the apartment above the candy shop. She pulled open the building door and climbed a freshly painted staircase, smothered by a stale chemical smell. She pounded on Kayla's door. She was waiting for her, of course with her sleepy morning smile. "I made coffee," she said. "Stef is on her way."

"You told her?"

"Yeah. You doing all right?"

"I don't really want to talk about it."

Kayla nodded and poured them both coffee and then sat in silence. Sometimes silence was all Paul needed to open up, but she stayed quiet. For Kayla, The Restlessness was always worst when it was silent. "Did I ever tell you about how I knew I needed to break up with my ex? One morning, he'd totally transformed overnight, isn't that weird? His mouth looked different. Like his father's or mine, or even like my own mouth. When you first love someone, it's like their whole face is so particular or something. His mouth and nose and eyes were the best I'd ever seen. But it all changed. They became so ordinary."

"Did you break up with him?"

"Well, I don't even know why, but I stayed. I just always stayed in things I didn't like back then . . . I was living with him way too long, two years too long, I lived with my parents too long, I stayed in school too long, and now just have a damn desk job out of it. I thought if I stayed, if I fulfilled my obligations I'd, I don't know, that it'd be worth it or something. But it never was. I thought I loved him and then I woke up and realized I didn't. I couldn't even stand to have him touch me." Someone knocked at the inside door. "Stef," Kayla said when Paul jumped. She went to open the door.

"Holla," called Paul from the kitchen.

Stef came in, went to the cupboard and grabbed herself a mug for coffee.

"Paul doesn't want to talk about it," said Kayla. "So I'm just telling her a bunch of garbage about my last breakup."

"It's not garbage," said Paul. "I want to know."

"We were talking about obligation and the terrible things it makes us do."

"Right," said Stef, and she stared into her coffee cup. "Do you have a little cream or milk?" Without waiting for an answer, Stef went to the fridge.

"What I really think," Kayla continued, "is that love and relationships and all that shouldn't be about possession or obligation, but about making a choice. And it's making that choice again and again that yes, I want to be with that person. That's my person. When I wake up in the morning, I choose my guy, he's still mine, and I'm still his, but that's not about possession, it's about caring for each other."

"I'm sorry, Kayla, but I don't think you're right," Stef said and dumped milk into her coffee.

"I'm just trying to say that Paul's not wrong for breaking up with him, even though she thinks he needs her to take care of him."

"I agree with that. But I think obligation is important. I mean, it's easy to talk about it when kids aren't involved. I know you guys never have to think about it, but it's a big deal to some of us around here."

"Stef, I'm not meaning to upset you. I just want Paul to feel a little better. Maybe you're right. Maybe I'm not thinking about all sides. What do I know, anyway? He's only my second really serious relationship. That's all. It's nothing."

Paul stopped listening and wandered around the apartment. Stef and Kayla would go on like this forever. Her phone was going off in her hand, texts from her degenerate, telling her she'd made a big mistake.

7.

Wind wasn't content with this, Paul safe away at Kayla's where the degenerate could no longer hurt her, only a few loose memories connecting them, memories that would, she hoped, fade as the years moved forward and she maybe found another love and built a life that didn't involve him. Wind couldn't have this. It brought a warm front in and dropped the temperature down. The degenerate, alone in the apartment, no one left to tell him to take his pills, stopped all together. He needed Paul, how could she leave, she thought she was better than him, where was she, he'd find where she was staying and show her she had no power over him, she was obviously breaking up with him to try to control him as usual, trying to show him that she was powerful, he didn't have the money to even stay in the apartment but it was his now, where was she, he had to find her to show her, he loved her so much, he needed to teach her that she wasn't right, that she didn't know what she was dealing with, he thought she had understood the magic of his thoughts, that he was special, she had told him he was special but now seemed to have forgotten, so he was going to have to find her to show her, how could she leave him, where was Paul, why wasn't she here, she had left him, how could she, he had to find her. Wind howled and built and howled, the warmth making it bold. It had more surprises in store, a storm, and next it was coming for Kayla.

8.

What Kayla had said about making the choice every day was true. She did wake up and make the choice, thought of Cam, and then stayed with the degenerate. This still did not solve the problem of Cam. He started texting her daily.

Her degenerate, off for the winter from his landscaping job, spent the days watching TV and then the nights finding drugs or watching TV and doing drugs, and Kayla had gotten bored of drugs and didn't even have a television at her apartment. But in the mornings beside her degenerate, Kayla felt the most love she thought she'd ever felt, like little doors opening and opening and opening. But this was all while the degenerate slept, never speaking.

After work one day, she went to see Cam, who she'd not seen since the night at The Cave, only texting. She went home and changed out of her work clothes. She pulled on a low-cut sweater dress and tights. Something between date and friends hanging out. She paused by her mirror and put on lipstick. Then she peeled off her tights and changed into her nice lace underwear, tights on again. The air warm as she walked.

The sidewalk was caked in slush, and Kayla jumped through it, spraying slush everywhere. Her phone vibrated in her pocket. Her degenerate was calling. "Hello?"

"Babe, what's up?"

"I'm just heading out for dinner. With Cam. We're going to The Cave. Where you at?"

"Just Cam?"

"I don't know, a few people might come out. I would have invited you, but I thought you were seeing Amir tonight."

"Yeah, I am. Just wanted to see what time you're coming by tonight."

"Like eleven? Maybe later. Depends who all is out."

"Okay. I might pass out there. Text him if you don't hear from me."

"Sure."

"Love you, babe."

Those doors that opened in her in the morning had all shut. "You too."

She cut down a side street, lined with townhomes. A cat was perched on a wet stone at the foot of a driveway. He meowed as she approached. Normally, she would engage a cat she passed in conversation, giving it a hello and asking it about its day. But Kayla wasn't herself. She had fancy underwear on and was ignoring a cat. She was lying to her boyfriend, who just this morning she had thought she loved fully. The cat walked beside her along the street, meowing softly. He was ginger, collarless, and a patch of his hair was missing, the skin there scarred. Where the street ended, the cat sat. She finally acknowledged him. "Thank you for escorting me," she said. The cat meowed again and flopped on his side in the slush. Kayla bent down and pet what little fur was dry on his stomach and then left him at the street corner, where he licked his paws. Maybe she hadn't woken up different. Kayla was still in there. She was there.

At The Cave, she drank too much and she and Cam forgot to go somewhere to eat. They had ordered beers and shots and cocktails. Cam ordered a Blow Job and a Muff Diver and a Polar Bear, laughing with the bartender every time. When it was time to pay, Cam said, "I've got this."

Kayla said, "No, let's split it. We're friends."

"Are we?" said Cam and raised his eyebrows, his eyes giving that mischievous flash. She dug through her wallet. She knew she had some money. She checked the other pocket. She looked through her coat, the rest of her purse.

"That bastard!"

"What is it?"

"I took out a hundred dollars yesterday."

"Did you spend it?"

"No, I haven't gone out since."

"Well, where would it have gone?"

"Seriously, Cam? Just think about it for a moment."

"Oh. Shit." Cam sat there, looking at his hands. "Well, I've got this, okay?"

"Sorry, I didn't expect this." But she should have. She whipped on her jacket. She forgot about the soggy warmth outside and bundled up fully in her hat, scarf, and gloves. They left the bar. Kayla immediately started to sweat once they were outside.

"So, did he take the money for drugs, do you think?"

"Yeah, probably. God, I'm so fucking pissed."

"Yeah, that sucks. I can't imagine doing that."

"Let's take the side streets. I need to see some beautiful

Toronto houses. Maybe that will calm me down. It pisses me off because if he needed money, I'd give him money. I'd lend him money or even just let him have it. He knows that. I give him things all the time. It's not a big deal. But he didn't even ask, he just took it from my wallet when I was over there. So it's obviously not just about needing the money."

"What do you think it's about?"

"I don't know. Having one over on me. Or something." She had thought tonight was the night she and Cam might kiss, that was what the texts and hanging out one-on-one was building toward, sleeping together, but right now, she just wanted to walk and talk. All her lust was gone now that she was caught up in her degenerate's betrayal. "I wonder if this is the first time. I'd kinda noticed that I always had less money in my wallet than I thought. But this is definitely the first time he totally cleaned me out like that."

"Do you think he wants to be caught?"

"Why would he want that?"

"Like a self-sabotage thing. One time I was seeing this girl I really liked, well, not seeing, but you know, fucking, and I got freaked. I don't know why. I liked her too much or something. Anyway, I started texting this other girl, this really raunchy stuff, and then I 'accidentally' sent a text with the other girl's name in it to the girl I really liked."

"Cam! Why would you do that?"

"I regret it now! I was scared!"

"Don't you know how you made that girl feel?"

"Well, we stopped seeing each other, obviously."

"You never send me raunchy texts."

Cam reached out to Kayla and put his arm around her shoulders. This was going to be the moment they kissed, Kayla knew it. "Well, Kayla, as you've said yourself, we're friends." He let her go and crossed the street, waiting for her to follow.

They came to the side street by Kayla's house and the cat walked up again. "Hey! Check out that cat!" Cam got down and patted his face. The cat arched his back, purring when Cam's hand went over the scarred bald spot. "What happened to you, old fella?"

"Cam," Kayla said, "never ask about scars. It's rude."

"You ever notice Paul's scars?"

"Of course."

"What are they from?"

"I've never asked. I told you, it's rude."

"Probably from a fistfight with a shark."

"You're so dumb." The cat walked alongside them. "Do you think he has a home?"

"He doesn't look it. That there is a streetcat. I'd know a streetcat anywhere."

"What's he going to do when it gets colder? Do you think he'll die?"

"It's a possibility. But he looks like a survivor to me." He walked them along the street, pressing against Cam's legs from time to time. "He's very polite."

"He likes you a lot. He walked me down to see you

too." They turned back onto Kayla's street and left the grizzled cat behind, and walked to her apartment. The candy shop. "Well, here we are," she said.

"Yep," said Cam and glanced at his phone. "Well, let me know how everything goes. I'm here for you, okay?"

"Yeah, I'll be okay." She started to pull open the door to her apartment staircase. There was no one else on the street, just the slushy night and flickering wind. "Hey, Cam," she called after him. He turned back around and waited. "I'm wearing my sexy underwear."

He laughed and waved, continuing down the street. Kayla went up and entered her apartment. She poked her head into the living room, where Paul was sleeping. Probably dreaming of fist fights with sharks, Kayla thought. Then she passed out in her bed. She'd deal with her degenerate tomorrow.

Doomsday, Kayla thought as she dressed for work the next morning. All day she refreshed emails, unable to concentrate on anything.

Her degenerate texted her around noon. **babe why didnt I here from u I came home afterall but you werent there thought youd come to my place after you were out??**

And another after she didn't reply. **u ok? how was last night**

On her lunch break, Kayla finally texted back. **I will come over tonight. Will you be there? I need to talk to you.**

ill be there

She thought of the cute way he'd smile at her, his lips

hiding his teeth, which he was self-conscious of, how he'd pull her into him at a party, how serious he could be with her. His stories about starting his own landscaping company when his father died, that time he'd almost been caught in a burning house (of course a fire he'd started). But she also thought about how gross it was when he was fucked up, that he was stealing her money to get fucked up. Sometimes he lied about how many drugs he did or which drugs he did. Some made him a little too scary, made his whole pupil and iris turn black and flat. Always loved dark eyes, drawn to darkness, hoping to be a light.

He was waiting for her at his place, sitting at the kitchen table, a joint burning on the table in front of him. Kayla grabbed a cigarette and lit it. If he was smoking inside, she would too. She wished her nerves were steadier. "So, what's this all about?" she said. "You're taking my money now?"

"Seriously, babe, is this why you're over here? To fight?"

"I don't get it. I'd give you whatever you want."

"Why do you think I've been taking your money? Anyone can walk in here at anytime, babe. Door's always open. You shouldn't leave your purse around."

"You're seriously going to lie right now? I can't keep doing this."

"Sure, babe. You won't be able to stay away. You think you'll ever be able to find what we have again?" Kayla's degenerate started to pull on his coat. He smiled at her, that smile that always ate her up. "Don't forget, babe, I know where you live." The degenerate left his house walking out where wind met him, pushing against his back on his way to Amir's.

9.

For a moment, Toronto was still. Paul's degenerate smoked outside of the apartment in Roncesvalles, the smoke not yet escaping his lips. Up near Bloor, Kayla's degenerate paused on his way to Amir's. Paul stared at a puzzle scattered across Kayla's living room table, her eyes searching for the piece to complete the Toronto Island skyline. Stef leaned against the wall in her house, a hand pressed to her forehead as she waited for Derek to walk through the door. As Wynn lay in bed, behind her eyes a darkness grew on the edge of sleep. Derek tried not to move, so he wouldn't wake *her, her* arms around his shoulders, *her* lips against his chest. Even Kayla, who would normally skid home along the ice and slush, was still, waiting before she pulled open the apartment door, looking down the road for a walking figure who would not come. The storm was already gathering along North America's west coast, and like every being it was waiting. Wind swept through and pushed the warm front east.

Kayla's apartment had been impenetrable. She'd never been scared of anyone really, except maybe a passing stranger on the street. Her parents were both good people, her father was gentle and sweet to her and her sister.

They'd even been disciplined halfheartedly, her parents not wanting to crush her positive spirit. There had been no monsters in Kayla's life. She sent distant but tender Facebook messages with her ex-boyfriend to check in with each other.

Now when Kayla returned after seeing the degenerate, every dark window had a face in it, she could feel wind creeping in, all the gaps in her apartment that could be easily forced through. Why hadn't she ever tested the locks? At least she'd never given him keys. Hello, hello, she thought, hello spectres in the windows, hello danger, here you are, finally. She hadn't been searching, but now that it was here, the possibility of the degenerate doing something stupid, the cost of having that sort of unpredictable person in her life, she was ready to face it head on. She peed in the washroom, smiled at herself in the mirror. That ol' Kayla face didn't look so innocent anymore.

Paul's degenerate woke her, talking in his sleep, threatening the man who attacked him in his nightmares. He shared Paul's night terrors, at times defending her when she was being attacked, or on a crusade all his own. She willed herself awake - sometimes he struck out in sleep and she wanted to move out of the way, or to help wake him, hold his limbs while he thrashed as she eased him into wakefulness. She opened her eyes. Above her, the plaster swirls of Kayla's ceiling. Kayla's musty spare pillow under her head. The man's voice didn't quite sound like

Paul's degenerate. His speech was always so pressured. This voice sloppily rolled along so that Paul couldn't understand from the living room. She got up and wandered to Kayla's bedroom. The voice was louder. She knocked. "Come in," Kayla called. "I'm awake."

Kayla was curled on her bed with her phone in her hands. Her degenerate's voice was playing from a voicemail. "I'm gonna come over there. I need to talk to you and you won't answer my calls. I don't know why you're being like this. I just want to talk to you."

"Don't let him come over," Paul said and climbed into her bed.

"Oh, definitely not. He left me three messages. He called while I was at work, of course I didn't answer. Then he called at nine and again at ten, he started leaving messages in the middle of the night. That he was going to come to the house. It's like, Give it up, buddy. We weren't even dating that long. Stef's on her way over too. Wynn has jazz or tap or something this morning, but she can't get ahold of Derek."

"No way."

"Yeah, I guess he just never came home last night. Here, listen to this." Kayla pressed play on the next message.

"Kayla, I know it's late, so I'm just going to come by and see if you're there. I'm just going to look for the lights, and if the lights aren't on, I'll go away, but I'm just going to knock and if you let me in, you let me in." The degenerate was slurring his words so heavily, Paul could barely understand him. Kayla groaned and put her head on Paul's shoulder.

"I texted Cam and told him about it, and he said that if anything happened, he'd be over here so fast and bury him. That's what he actually said."

"Cam's such a little thing though."

"Yeah, but he's tough. He could do it. Especially if I was threatened."

"He wouldn't do anything though, right?"

"I honestly don't know. I never know with him. He could do anything and I wouldn't be surprised."

Stef called Kayla's phone, asking her to come unlock the downstairs door, and Kayla left Paul in her bed. Paul scrolled through the texts from her degenerate, begging to know where she was staying. Stef and Kayla came in, and Stef flopped at the foot of Kayla's bed. Kayla climbed back in too. "So, Derek finally called me. He says he was at a friend's. That he fell asleep."

Paul glanced at Kayla and shook her head. Now wasn't the time to talk about her. "Well, at least he didn't come here last night. That's something. Hopefully this means that he won't," Kayla said.

Paul's phone buzzed in her hand. Her degenerate's name displayed across the screen. "Don't answer it," Kayla said.

"She's right. Let it ring through. See if he leaves a message," Stef said. Kayla slid to the foot of her bed and gave Stef a hug.

The phone buzzed and buzzed. Finally it stopped. It

buzzed twice and lit up with a missed-call alert. "What are the chances?" Kayla said. "All three of us? How fucked is that?"

Wind howled outside, rattling Kayla's bedroom window. Stef's phone dinged with a text from Derek. She paused to read it. "Well, he's finally back home."

"When are you going to kick him out, Stef?" asked Kayla. "Seriously."

"It's complicated," Stef said. She sat up and stood, started folding Kayla's blankets, kicked to the floor. "I can't."

"Just, if it was me, he'd already be gone. That's all I'm saying. He's not pulling his weight, he's not there for you the way he used to be. You aren't happy, and you have so much going for you. It bugs me to see you treated like this."

"Give it a rest, Kayla," said Paul. "You don't know how it is."

"Sorry if not all of us want to hop on the breakup train, Kayla," Stef said. She sent another text.

Paul's phone buzzed again, with a text this time. **paul stop avoiding me**

And another one. **I will find where you are**

And another. **babe ill never forget you**

I'll never forget you, the degenerates sang in unison into wind, cigarettes in their mouths and static in their brains. I'll never forget you and I'll find you, spend the rest of my days, haunted by you, by us. The degenerates flickered in the memories of Kayla, Stef, and Paul, and joined into one terrorizing figure, lurking at the edges of their nightmares, like wind - able to go anywhere, bringing destruction with it.

Many nights that week Kayla spent with Cam, finally finding her way into his bed. The more nights she spent with him, the more she yearned for the touch of her degenerate. Kayla wished she could have two hearts in her. If she did, one would always feel for Cam. It would beat slowly and evenly, no beat out of place.

When she had sex with Cam, part of her floated away out the window, became one of the spectres looking for other people, she felt cold in her chest, and her body took over, pure sensation. Afterwards, as he whispered to her about how he thought that she was so cool and that maybe she'd be the girl for him after all this time, her spectre-self roamed the streets of Toronto, searching for her streetcat, her degenerate, any crushes from the past. She tried to muster up all of the affection she'd ever felt for the world and channel it into Cam, but she was aware that with the toughness that had blossomed in her over night, an emptiness or numbness, was also growing.

Paul received a couple nervous calls from her degenerate's parents wondering if she'd heard from him. He'd disappeared off of social media and they were making sure his bills were paid, but weren't sure where he was. She'd told them about the text messages, the threats and promises, the calls, and they begged her that if he called again, she would pick up and tell him to get in touch with them, then she was to call them right away. If they didn't hear from him, they were going to come into Toronto from Sudbury on the weekend, even with the big storm that was supposed to hit. "What big storm?" asked Paul.

"Didn't you hear?" the degenerate's mother told her. "It's a severe weather warning. The few days right before Christmas. Make sure you have a flashlight and blankets. Power will probably go out."

"Oh, I'll have to tell Kayla."

"Kayla?"

"Yeah, my friend I've been staying with." Why had she said that? She never told anyone anything. Never trusted. How had she been lulled into trusting his mother, telling her where she was? "I have to go."

"Well, you'll pick up if he calls? You'll tell him to call me?"

"Yes, yes, I have to go."

Paul hung up the phone. The degenerate didn't call her again. He no longer had to.

10.

That night at The Cave, The Man Paul Used To Love/Still Loved bought her a drink. They stood away from their friends: Kayla sitting beside Cam, looking out the window and remembering the degenerate who had caught snow in his lashes; Cam looking at Kayla and knowing she would always be looking elsewhere; Steph checking her phone for texts from Derek and the sitter; her other friends drifting in and out of the cold to puff on cigarettes and moan about their lives, forgetting to feel for a moment how everything bumped up against everything else, collision after collision, a perfect thing. "I heard about the breakup," The Man She Used To Love/Still Loved Said, sipping his drink quickly.

She shrugged. "How have you been?" She crept a hand towards his, his long fingers curved around his pint glass. For once, he didn't pull his hand away. He kept it steady where it was, neither reaching out to her nor retracting.

"Busy," he said. "But thinking."

"Writing?"

"Of course. And you? Still teaching those kids their colours at that art program?"

"And about empathy and beauty, yes, I am."

"Good. We need people who appreciate beauty." They stood together, the back of her fingers still touching the back of his. "Want another drink?" he asked.

"Sure," she said.

"Don't get all crazy drunk though."

Paul pulled her hand away. He shot the rest of his beer down and winked at her. "You're always such a jerk to me."

He stepped closer. She was faced with his chest, and he peered down at her. "The other night, when we were walking, I meant what I was saying. I mean, not all of that other stuff. We always drive each other wild, I don't know why."

"You know why."

"Maybe I do. But that stuff, about anything that happens to you . . ."

"Being important to you."

"Well, it is. And I'm glad to see that you're in a better place, and I'm glad that I'm able to buy you another drink. You'll have another drink with me?"

"Fine."

"And you're not even that bad of a drunk."

"Really?" They both laughed at this.

"Most of the time."

They had another drink together, talking easily for once. At the end of the night, they waved bye as if they were old friends, finally old friends, happy to see each other. Rain began to fall.

11.

The ice storm came. Wind carried in the warm front and then a cold front, and the rain fell and froze and coated all the trees with ice. The ice built in layers, crackling and smooth. Wind pressed it into alcoves, the nooks of tree branches. The water went into cracks in wood and then the temperature dropped even more and the water froze, the ice smashing apart trees. The ancient tree with the plaque lost branch after branch, falling to the ground. The world was grey and glistening, soggy and slick.

Paul's degenerate needed to find her. He'd finally spoken to his mother, and she had told him he just needed to take care of himself, maybe to come home for a rest.

"Don't worry about Paul," she said. "She's staying with Kayla. I'm sure those girls are doing just fine together."

"With Kayla?" he said. Why hadn't he thought of Kayla's? His thoughts were always moving too fast for him to properly focus. Idiot. Of course, Kayla's. He'd go there. Somehow it was now the middle of the night and he'd been off the phone for hours but he didn't know how he'd lost track of time. But he remembered Kayla's. It was raining, icy rain, he hated rain, and it was slippery. He skidded along the street in his shoes, and there was the candy shop. The front door was locked. The windows were dark. He banged on the door, but with the staircase going up to the inside door, there was no way in. Then he remembered the back door. Of course. Genius to have remembered. He walked down the street to the alley that cut behind all of the buildings on her street until he was at the back of Kayla's. He climbed the fire escape. His shoe slipped on one of the steps and he caught himself. He thought about pounding on the back door, but he remembered the face Paul used to make when she was really scared. How she sucked at her bottom lip. Twisted her hair in her fingers, strands finding their way into her mouth. He sat on the iron steps as the ice-rain came down. His hair was matted to his head. There weren't too many hours until morning. He could wait. He didn't have anything else to do. He could wait.

"Um, there's someone outside," one of Kayla's roommates said in the morning.

"No," Kayla said. "Shit." She peered outside. Mist clouded the air, and each surface reflected light leaking through the grey. Halfway down the fire escape, a man lay limp. "Paul!"

She was already awake, she already knew, she was outside so quickly. "Call 9-1-1!" she told Kayla.

"The cops?"

"Ambulance!"

Paul went out onto Kayla's porch, slicked with ice and instantly fell. She knew she would be bruised by the fall, felt the pain in her butt and knees, but she had to get down the stairs. She slid herself over to the railing and pulled herself up. Sheets of ice broke off the black iron as she gripped it, skidding over to the stairs. There was no way she'd be able to walk down them without falling, so Paul slid. She held onto the railing's metal bars and stuck her legs out flat, letting herself slide down one step at a time, until she reached her sleeping degenerate, peacefully drifting into a hypothermic sleep. Paul wrapped her body around him. She pressed her skin to his cold face, her cheek against his cheek. Kayla tossed her a blanket from the porch, which caught in wind and almost missed the staircase altogether. Paul managed to grab a corner and pulled it over to her degenerate. She tucked it around him. She brushed the ice from his hair, his face, his jacket. "Hey, baby," she said as his eyes fluttered. "Don't worry, I'm here."

He opened his eyes. "It's you," he said.

"Yeah, it's me. I wasn't about to let you freeze to death."

He clung to her as she heard the ambulance approach, its wail nearer every moment.

It became something else people just say. Where were you when the ice storm hit? Did you hear the trees splitting? Did your power go out, plunging you into blackness? And then what did you see in the dark?

Before the power went out, Kayla ordered three sets of pepper spray as Christmas presents. This was getting ridiculous. A man passed out on her staircase, one of her friends stranded in her living room. Stef had heard from Derek that Kayla's degenerate had been walking past her apartment daily, looking for lights in the windows. He'd told him not to do that, it was better for him to stay away. Sure, Derek wasn't giving Stef too much trouble, even though everyone knew about *her*, but the ones you cared about could flip on you so easily. Well, hello, beautiful people! Hello hello, beautiful, dangerous people! Hello! Hello! Hello! Kayla ordered rush delivery.

Kayla had watched Paul hold a man that she claimed to no longer love, to have possibly never loved, watched her hop in the ambulance beside him and head off to the hospital where she'd wait with him until his parents made it in from Sudbury. He'd go back in the hospital for a while this time, Kayla thought, even though Paul had hoped he'd never go back there. Kayla couldn't imagine doing something like that for her degenerate, now that they'd split up. She must have never really loved someone, she was like Cam, or maybe she was also finally a degenerate. No feeling except for what others could do for you. There were only degenerates, looking for their saviours, looking to the sky and seeing nothing and then looking to other degenerates instead.

Stef came by with Wynn, taking a cab slowly through the storm, the streetcars frozen on their tracks. They set Wynn up with a movie in the living room, and Stef told Kayla that, once again, she couldn't get through to Derek. Christmas was just a few days away, and now that her mother was gone, Stef liked to stay in Toronto with Derek and Wynn and have a family celebration, but he was missing. "I'm sure he got stuck somewhere with the ice, that's it."

"This isn't the first time this has happened, Stef."

"So what, you think it's drugs?"

Kayla put on some hot water for tea. It was finally time. "Stef, there's someone else. Maybe more than one."

"Fuck, again? What am I supposed to do about it this close to Christmas?" Stef stared out the window at the icy fire escape. She watched the snow now coming down to dust the ice. "Everything will be fine." Stef remembered another Christmas, where it was just her, alone with Wynn, Wynn's father gone. Stef had bundled Wynn up and brought her to her mother's house, where they talked about when Stef's father had left. And her mother had told her, that it got easier eventually. Stef hadn't known what she meant, and then the next year, she had met Derek. She worried about Wynn losing Derek, but Wynn seemed aware most days that it was her and Stef building their own world.

"Well, I've never experienced anything like this before. I don't have a clue."

"They just become things that happen to you. And you move on, Kayla."

"But what if it changes you?"

"I always thought that was a good thing."

Stef and Wynn would go home when the movie was over, and she'd get Wynn excited for Christmas and explain to her that Derek would no longer live with them. She'd hold her if she needed to be held, she'd talk to her if she needed to talk, she'd play with her if she felt like she needed a friend. When Derek came back, as he would, well, maybe she'd let him come back and maybe she wouldn't. It would depend on what he had to say, but finally, Stef would talk to him. The lights flickered, and then completely went out. Kayla grabbed blankets for the three of them and they joined Wynn on the couch. They told Wynn a story. Stef called her Wynnita, and she pressed into her mother as she heard the nickname. The story was about a storm: there was lightning and wind that constantly made things worse, trees were broken, even people's favourite trees, but in the morning, the storm was over, and all the lights came back on.

12.

In Caledon, Paul walked through the forest, encased in

ice. The stillness broken by the gentle creak then snap as branches collapsed.

Another crack shot off in the distance. The degenerate would be lying in his hospital bed, hoping he'd be able to get a three-day pass for Christmas. She hadn't thought it would come to this. She had wanted to help him. Kayla told her again and again how brave she'd been. Paul appreciated that, she really did, but wondered if his relapse was all her fault.

At home, her father was making a fire for her. The roads were dangerous and the power kept blacking out, so they might need it to heat the house too. Her mother had stockpiled candles. They were so resourceful, true adults. Paul picked up a branch and knocked it against the trunk of a tree. Ice fell from the branches. She smacked it and smacked it and eventually just threw the branch away, she could feel that familiar feeling again, rising up in her, her fists balled up in her gloves, she needed to hit something, it'd feel good to hit something and hear the splintering ice around her, to have branches fall all around her as she lashed out, how steady and silent everything was compared to Toronto, her wonderful Caledon trees frozen and still. Breathe in. Count to four. Breathe out. Count to four. Breathe in. Count to five. Breathe out. Count to five. Keep going. Her hands unballed. She looked straight up at the pattern the icy branches made against the sky. Breathe in. Count to six. Breathe out. Count to six. Breathe in.

Back in Toronto, after Christmas, Kayla walked to meet

Cam. It'd be impossible to explain everything to him about the ice storm. He thought the situation with their degenerates was clear: Never speak to them again. And yes, sometimes she agreed.

A man walked in front of her, carefully along the slick sidewalk. She recognized his olive-green jacket, broad shoulders, hair hidden by toque. The hair, straight, black and long. She knew when he turned around, as he would, he must, he'd hear her heart burning up - he could sense The Restlessness, the way he had that first night in the attic apartment - she'd be able to see his lashes, his mouth, he'd give her that smile. Was he looking for her? Was that why he was out here? And he did turn, but the face was half-covered in beard, the eyes blue, not her degenerate. She hadn't heard from him in days.

A cat crept out from in between two snowbanks, meowing faintly. "It's you!" she said to her ginger friend. "I thought you would've died in the storm." The cat gave her a steady blink. She got down on the icy sidewalk. The cat's ear had split, and one fang was missing and one now protruded forward. Kayla examined him, checking to see if the tooth was loose, that his ear wasn't bleeding. He purred and flopped on his side, showing her his belly, his ribs. "All right, you're coming with me," she said and brought him back to the apartment. She sent a quick text to Cam to cancel and put out tuna for her new degenerate. He knew what the streets were like. He meowed at Kayla and jumped in her lap. She pet his head. "I know!" said Kayla to his meows. "It's fucking hard out there!"

Paul knew the way to his house by heart. Stacks of branch-es littered the street, waiting to be collected. She didn't even know if he'd be home, but she couldn't call him, not out of the blue like this. She could drop by his house, just like a degenerate would, she could find him. Come out, my love, Paul wanted to howl, Come out and find me! But instead she went to the townhouse he lived in, its trees all bent and broken, pulled open the front door, and climbed up to the top-floor apartment. She knocked on his door. She could hear the scrape of his chair pushing away from the table, she counted the footsteps it took him to reach the door and open it. "Paulina," he said. "I didn't know you were back in Toronto already."

"Well, here I am."

"Want to come in?"

He poured her some coffee from a pot he'd made. He poured milk in it, the way she liked it. He had a word-processing document open on his laptop, and he shut it, cleared off the table for them to sit. They sat across from each other in silence. "Did you lose power?" she asked.

"Yeah, for a bit. I went to visit my dad over Christmas, but I lost it a bit before then. On the 22nd and 23rd."

"Yeah. It kept going out in Caledon." She never knew what to say him. It had been so easy at The Cave, like they were starting over, but here they were, still not able to speak to each other.

"So, how come you're here? Today . . ."

His hands were shaking as he lifted the cup to his mouth. Had he always shaken around her? She couldn't remember. That year with the degenerate had erased many things she'd always remembered about people. She guessed you could be so solely focused on one person that the rest drifted away. "I've been wanting to talk to you for a while, actually. About everything that happened last year with us. I wasn't in a good place, and then you had a boyfriend, and there never was the right time to talk to you."

She remembered two heartbroken summers ago, she remembered a heartbroken fall. "All right. We can talk."

"I guess I just wanted to check in on your feelings, or whatever."

"My feelings?"

"Yeah, about all that stuff that happened between us."

She wanted to tell him that there was a week she'd thought she was pregnant, back when they'd been sleeping together. Wanted to be pregnant. She wanted to tell him about how she'd wandered around the city all summer and all fall looking for someone who could ease the pain from his push and pull, the pain of her past, the pain of another hard thing that happened that summer, until she'd found her degenerate. And it wasn't that she blamed The Man She Used To Love/Still Loved for this, she didn't. She knew the three of them had been blown about, their actions not entirely their own. "What do you want me to say?"

"What?"

"Tell me what you want me to say, and I'll say it. I'll say whatever you fucking want."

"Why are you angry? I don't get you. I'm trying to be nice."

"I'm a tree covered in fucking ice. I'm splitting down the middle and branches are falling everywhere. I'm made of cracked branches, and people from the city are coming to cut them down because they're a hazard."

"I don't get you at all."

"I really don't know what you want from me."

"You're always calling me Paulina, and everyone calls me Paul."

He stood up and walked around the room, his hands threaded together on top of his head. "I think I'm in love with you, all right?"

She tried to do her breathing exercise, but sitting at his table, with that coffee he'd made her, she couldn't remember the counting. She grabbed her bag and stood to go.

The street, the icy street, she could walk the streets of Toronto forever. She kicked at snowbanks, built up over the ice, as she went. She knew if there was something looking down on her, the way Kayla thought and even Stef, it wouldn't be happy with her unless it was the devil. Paul imagined if there was anything up there, it might be kind of like her and all of these people she knew stumbling their way through the world. She glared up at the sky where a sun glared back. If I'm bad, dear sun, then so are you. The sun blazed in a blue sky, after the storm, at peace.

That night, in another part of the city, people were climbing on rooftops, trying not to slip, watching for satellites that tricked stars in the sky. They were at parties, they knew how to dance. They smoked on porches and talked about their childhoods, they talked about their recent pasts. They dreamed of places they would one day live, far away from Toronto, in a country they would make their own. They witnessed crimes. They met other people and saw themselves in each other, reflected. They were drawn together, repelled apart. They had wounds that wouldn't heal, they discovered things about their health. They would never be cured. They loved other people, so many people, they yearned and grew. They lied frequently. They promised. They made wishes, and all was still, no matter what their names were, not promising anything in return.

Wind blew snow across the December sky, dreams of a better place caught along with it. Kayla and Paul and Stef walked through Toronto streets, pepper spray in their pockets, praying to a god they weren't sure existed that they wouldn't have to use it on someone they loved.

Acknowledgments

Many teachers guided me over the years. Thank you to Mrs. Harrison, Matt Chevalier, Ron Lanteigne, Toby Cadham, Frank Pozzuoli, Jennifer Keyes, and Laurie L.H. for letting me do my own thing and telling me to keep going. And much thanks to my fiction mentors and workshop leaders who both encouraged me and kicked my ass, whichever I needed most: Margo Swiss, Shyam Selvadurai, David Layton, Michael Helm, Rosemary Sullivan, Michael Winter, Richard Greene, and Michael Redhill.

Many friends and peers helped to shape this book along the way and act as some of my first readers, providing edits, guidance, and a fresh look. Thank you to my first readers: Sofia Mostaghimi, Nadia Ragbar, Andrew Battershill, Cheryl Runke, Menaka Ramen-Wilms, Joe Thomson, Alex Lussier-Craig, and my peers from creative writing at York University and the University of Toronto. Thank you Spencer Gordon and Kevin Hardcastle for your advice and guidance during the publication process.

To editors of the past, Kathryn Mockler, Jesse Eckerlin, Adam Zachary: Thank you for helping to make *Pauls* better and getting the stories into print. And especially thank you to Emily M. Keeler; I owe everything to you.

Thank you to my family for their support and inspiration. Marilyn Boyle-Taylor and John Taylor, you are the most interesting people I've met. Also thank you to Kenny and Beata Taylor.

Some of these stories have been in print before. "Multicoloured Lights" was published in the 2015 Summer issue of *CNQ*. "We Want Impossible Things" was featured on

Joyland in June 2015, and "Claire's Fine" was in the 2015 Spring issue of *The Hart House Review*. "Paul" and "Breakfast Curry" were both published in *Little Brother Magazine*, No. 3 and No. 6, respectively. "Paul" was also published as part of The National Magazine Awards 37th Gold Book.

Thank you also to the Toronto Arts Council, who provided support for the writing of *Pauls* and made my life financially viable.

Finally, thank you to Hazel Millar, Jay Millar, Malcolm Sutton, and Rick Meier. BookThug feels like a family, and thank you for all the hard work and long hours you put in to make *Pauls* exist.

Colophon

Distributed in Canada by the Literary Press Group:
www.lpg.ca

Distributed in the United States by Small Press Distribution:
www.spdbooks.org

Shop online at www.bookthug.ca

Edited for the press by Malcolm Sutton
Copy edited by Ruth Zuchter
Designed by Malcolm Sutton
Typeset in Yoga